IAN ALLEN

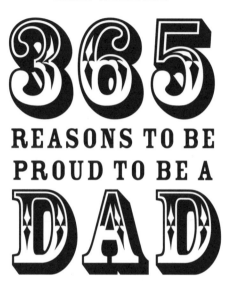

365

REASONS TO BE
PROUD TO BE A

DAD

PORTICO

To the three reasons I have to be proud to be a Dad –
Chris, Nick and Debbie.

First published in the United Kingdom in 2015 by
Portico
1 Gower Street
London
WC1E 6HD

An imprint of Pavilion Books Company Ltd

ISBN 978-1-91023-209-5

A CIP catalogue record for this book is available from
the British Library.

10 9 8 7 6 5 4 3 2 1

Reproduction by COLOURDEPTH
Printed and bound by 1010 Printing International Ltd, China

This book can be ordered direct from the publisher
at www.pavilionbooks.com

'Fatherhood is great because you can ruin someone from scratch.'

Jon Stewart

INTRODUCTION

When I was invited to write one of Portico's *365 Reasons ...* books, I jumped at the chance. Times are hard, after all. I began to wonder which of my many specialities was being called on. Would it be *365 Reasons to Love Football*, perhaps, or *365 Reasons Why Beer is Great*? Alas, no. You know exactly what they were looking for (unless you're in the habit of randomly picking up books and reading the introduction without looking at the title).

Three hundred and sixty-five reasons to be proud to be a Dad! Speaking as a Dad myself, that worried me – there is such a thing as the Trades Descriptions Act, as you'll find out in the entry for 30 November. Sixty-five, perhaps? No way. Five at a stretch. That's OK, they said, it can be a bit different from the other *365* books. Thank goodness.

So what you'll find inside this book is a collection of events that might make you appreciate being a Dad; some things that might make you think, 'It could be worse ...'; some that will remind you of just what Dads like; and some that will remind you of just what Dads *are* like. For each day of the year you'll find an interesting little vignette that in some way, however cryptic – tenuous is such an ugly word – will conjure up an image of Dad-dom and its attendant delights.

It will visit topics such as a Dad's favourite sports, cars, heroes, TV programmes and blighted ambitions, and drop in on one or two famous fathers down the ages. Some of the entries are, I admit, little more than an excuse to drag up an awful old Dad joke, some are an opportunity to drop in a fascinating factoid, and I must confess to having indulged one or two of my own private passions.

You'll discover the obvious Dad way of killing a rogue elephant; the world's first flying cow; and the beekeeping father of chiropractics who was run over by his irate son. You'll find out what a Pegasus crossing is, why it's not a good idea to accompany an army over a bridge, and where the world's first self-assembly furniture is.

If nothing else, by 31 December you'll have some idea of how a certain type of Dad thinks – but please don't be under any illusions that you'll then be any closer to understanding him. To paraphrase Lord Palmerston talking about Schleswig-Holstein, 'Only three people know the answer to the Dad question: one is dead, one is mad, and the third is me … and I've forgotten.'

JANUARY

PUT YOUR FEET UP

Dads have a hectic life, working, running around after the kids, going to the pub, etc., and it's not much more than a hundred years ago that a poor old Dad would have to work until he dropped or else throw himself on the mercy of his family or the workhouse. But on 1 January 1909 the Old Age Pensions Act took effect, and over half a million people aged 70 and over were eligible – providing they were of 'good character' – for payments of up to five shillings (25p) per week. Luxury!

WHAT'S IN A NAME?

On this day in 533 Pope John II took up his position as head of the Catholic Church. And what has this got to do with our subject, you might be asking? Well, before becoming John II, this Pope went by the moniker of Mercurius – named after a Roman god, so not ideal for a Pontiff – and so he became the first Holy Father to take a new papal name. And what Dad hasn't dreamed of making a fresh start by trading in his run-of-the-mill handle for a more macho, thrusting version? I quite fancy being a Dirk …

ANOTHER FEW SECONDS SAVED

Dads love labour-saving devices, so what a relief on this day in 1957 when the world's first battery-powered wristwatch was introduced. Admittedly, self-winding watches had been around for a bit before then: Abraham-Louis Perrelet's earliest device from 1777 worked on the same principle as a pedometer, with 15 minutes' walking required to wind it up (and what Dad wants to do that?). From the 1920s designs improved, but you still had to move your arm a bit. Admittedly the new watch wasn't brilliant at keeping time (that would have to wait for quartz watches a few years later), but for lazy Dads that was a minor drawback.

EDISON THE JUMBO KILLER

This is a sad tale and readers of a delicate disposition and animal-lovers may wish to look away now. Thomas Edison, despite having six children, found time to lodge over a thousand patents in his lifetime. But when Topsy the circus elephant was deemed a danger to her keepers after killing one (after years of abuse, it has to be said in her defence), Edison came up with an idea only a Dad would dream up – he decided electrocution was the answer. So in 1903 poor Topsy was fed a dose of cyanide-laced carrots before 6,600 volts finished her off. Anticipating YouTube, he filmed the event and, after much head-scratching, titled it *Electrocuting an Elephant*.

THE DANGERS OF NOT BEING A DAD

Despite living to what was then the grand old age of over 60, and being married for more than 20 years, Edward the Confessor never had kids. Historians are divided as to whether he was celibate, didn't much fancy his wife Edith, or whether there was just something funny in the water. Whatever the reason was, when he died childless on this day in 1066, the succession crisis opened up a huge can of worms that led to the Battle of Hastings and William the Conqueror's successful invasion later that year.

SECONDS OUT!

Dads are by nature a bit cowardly, but they're more than happy to watch two willing participants beat each other senseless for half an hour or so. The first recorded boxing match took place today in 1681 and was the brainchild of Christopher Monck, 2nd Duke of Albemarle. Not that he put himself in the firing line, heaven forbid. He got a couple of pugilistic plebs (his butler and butcher, actually) to knock seven bells out of one another while he (and presumably a group of his upper-class pals) watched and placed bets. The butler didn't do it this time, and the butcher slaughtered him.

PALINDROMIC DELIGHT

Although the first commercial traffic wouldn't pass through the Panama Canal until later in the year, on this day in 1914 the French crane boat *Alexandre La Valley* reached the Pacific Ocean. The much-delayed scheme had been started back in 1881 by the French, but was finally completed over 30 years later by the Americans. And including this feat here isn't a dig at Dads' DIY efforts that always have a similar deadline failure – it's an opportunity (all right then, an excuse) to repeat one of those fascinating palindromes Dads love to 'entertain' you with – 'A man, a plan, a canal: Panama!'

WHERE'S MY BACON BUTTY?

There's nothing most Dads like more than a bacon bap, melting butter oozing down their chins, accompanied by a nice cup of sweet tea. Heaven! So what is there to celebrate about this day in 1940 when the British Government announced the rationing of bacon, butter and sugar? It should have been a Dad disaster. But it was a sacrifice in the national interest during World War Two, and hence Dads could brace their stiff upper lips in true Trevor Howard style, despite being desperate for a good fry-up. Bread, curiously, remained un-rationed during the war, only to be limited for a two-year period from 1946.

WHY DON'T I-PHONE YOU?

9

On this day in 2007 Apple's Steve Jobs unveiled his latest shiny gadget designed to part Dads from their cash – the iPhone. With its touch-screen technology and all sorts of acronyms Dads pretend to know about, it has gone on to conquer the world of mobile phones, and the desperate efforts of competitors to keep up has led to huge choice in the smartphone marketplace. The iPhone, now on its seventh generation (though it will probably be its eighth or ninth by the time you read this), passed total sales of 500 million in March 2014 – most of them probably to replace ones that Dads have dropped down the toilet.

BEST DRINK OF THE DAY

No Dad is quite himself without his early-morning cuppa, and for that he can thank the enlightened Chinese emperor Shen Nung, who lived about 5,000 years ago. While his servants were boiling a pan of water for him to drink (he was a stickler for hygiene), some dried leaves from a *Camellia sinensis* bush fell into the pan and turned the water a funny brown colour.

Rather than flogging the servants for carelessness, as any emperor worth the name would, Shen Nung decided to drink it, and found it very refreshing. We don't know what date this happened, but we do know that the first London tea auction of Assam tea was held today in 1839, and that Britons now drink six billion cups of tea every year.

IT COULD BE YOU

What Dad hasn't dreamed of winning it big on the Lottery and blowing it all on madcap schemes like fast cars, big houses and buying his local football club? Roll back to 1567 and his Elizabethan counterpart would have been dreaming of buying a sophisticated carriage, a manor house and perhaps his local archery club as England's first state lottery offered a £5,000 prize for a ten-bob (50p) ticket. And that's not all – ticket purchasers were granted immunity from arrest for seven days, anticipating Monopoly's Get-Out-of-Jail-Free card by centuries.

TRUST YOU TO BRING US HERE

Three cheers for Octavia Hill, Robert Hunter and Hardwicke Rawnsley for forming the National Trust on this day in 1895. Without it, where would Dads be able to drag their complaining kids round on a wet Bank Holiday? The Trust owns 200 properties, many acquired in lieu of death duties in the mid-20th century. The very first property they bought, Alfriston Clergy House, was purchased for £10 in 1896 – it now costs £12 to take a family round it! Canny Dads buy a National Trust family membership and get in everywhere for free.

FIRST FOR FAAS

What a great day for Dads with 'musical' kids in 1854 when Philadelphia's Anthony Faas was granted the first patent for an accordion (a cross between a set of bagpipes and a Bullworker). Accordioning to the patent (sorry), as well as changing the keyboard, one of the improvements Faas made was to 'enhance the sound' – so God knows what it must have sounded like before! Incidentally, all Dads know what perfect pitch is – it's when you toss an accordion into a skip and it lands on a violin.

ROYAL CONNECTIONS

14 On this day in 1878 Queen Victoria was shown 'the operations of a telephone' by Alexander Graham Bell at Osborne House on the Isle of Wight. She exchanged niceties with Sir Thomas and Lady Biddulph at Osborne Cottage, listened to a rendition of 'Comin' thro' the Rye' from a young lady at the piano who happened to be with them, and later on had to endure an organ recital of the national anthem from London down the phone. It all makes Dads' 'I'm on the train' conversations seem quite exciting in comparison …

IT'S ON THE COMPUTER, IT MUST BE TRUE

15 Dads are great bluffers, so a website that enables people to speedily check up on their tall stories doesn't at first sight seem like a step forward. Wikipedia was launched today in 2001 by Jimmy Wales and Larry Sanger, the name being a combination of the Hawaiian word for quick (Wiki) and the end of encyclopedia. But the great thing about Wikipedia is that anyone can edit it – so canny Dads could still assure their kids that Winston Churchill ate a jar of pickled onions for breakfast every day, as long as they've made the change to Wiki first. Not that I'm encouraging any such thing, of course …

IS IT A BIRD? IS IT A PLANE?
OR JUST A CARTOON?

Superman had been around for a few years since being dreamed up by Jerry Siegel and Joe Shuster in 1933 (originally as a super-villain, interestingly), and first appeared in comic books in 1938. But on this day in 1939 he made his debut to a wider audience with a newspaper comic strip. Within a couple of years it was being syndicated to hundreds of publications; millions of readers became familiar with the adventures of the Man of Steel. And Dads everywhere had a new role model (in their dreams …).

GREAT SCOTT

Dads know all about heroic failures in everyday life, but one of the most poignant examples on a grander scale is commemorated today. In 1912 Captain Robert Falcon Scott and four colleagues reached the South Pole. They had hoped to be the first men ever to do so – instead they found they'd been beaten by the Norwegian Roald Amundsen by five weeks. 'The worst has happened,' recorded Scott. But in fact the worst was still to come, as all five perished on the homeward journey, leaving behind only Scott's moving words: 'Had we lived, I should have had a tale to tell … which would have stirred the heart of every Englishman.'

ANYONE FANCY A HAWAII?

Whatever reputation Dads have for blundering in somewhere and making a delicate situation worse, few of them could have done a worse job than Captain Cook on this day in 1778, when he landed on an archipelago of North Pacific islands and named them the Sandwich Islands – which must have come as a surprise to the roughly one million people who were living on the Hawaiian Islands at the time. But his pompous renaming was the least of their troubles – the British crew brought with them infectious diseases new to the islands, and within 50 years the population had shrunk to about 130,000.

THAT'S NOT A WORD!

In 1938 Alfred Butts from Poughkeepsie, New York, invented a board game that would sweep the world. He first called it Lexiko; soon, realising it needed a snappier name, he changed it to … Criss-Crosswords. Hmmm. For some reason it still didn't take off, but in 1948 James Brunot bought the rights and renamed it Scrabble. He was soon struggling to keep up with production and the major board-game players stepped in; on this day in 1955 the Spears company introduced the game to the UK, and Dads could start playing words like 'zolping' and daring their kids to challenge them.

HE MADE IT!

On this day in 1989, President Ronald Reagan officially left office. And what has that got to do with Dads? Well, nothing much, except we Dads love our fascinating facts, and when Ronnie left the White House intact, he became the first President who had been elected in a year ending in zero to survive office since James Monroe (elected 1820). In between Reagan and Monroe, four had been assassinated (Lincoln, Garfield, McKinley and Kennedy) and three died of natural causes (Harrison, Harding and Roosevelt). And Reagan nearly didn't make it – he was shot in 1981 and survived.

WHO LOVES YA, BABY

Happy birthday, Kojak! Telly Savalas was born on this day in 1922. Although this isn't a birthday book, let's make an exception for the man who helped make bald cool. Oddly, his brother George, who played Sergeant Stavros in *Kojak* opposite his sibling, had a fine head of hair. Telly was on the telly all through the 1970s, it seemed, and you can still catch *Kojak* being repeated now – though thankfully his awful recording of 'If' from 1975 doesn't get much airplay.

HEROES OF RORKE'S DRIFT

On 22 January 1879 a British and colonial force of just over 150 men isolated at the mission station of Rorke's Drift faced an onslaught from between 3,000 and 4,000 Zulus. The attack began at around 4pm and continued until the early hours of the next morning, by which time 17 of the defending force and over 350 Zulu warriors lay dead. The heroic stand has gone down in history – 11 Victoria Crosses were awarded for the action. And on the same day in 1964 the film *Zulu* was released, starring Stanley Baker and Michael Caine. Voted eighth in a list of Greatest War Films of all time, it's become a must-see for Dads.

IF I'VE GOT TO BE EMPEROR, SO HAVE YOU

Every Dad needs to know when to hand over some responsibility to his kids, but the Roman Emperor Theodosius I went a little too far on this day in AD 393 when he appointed his nine-year-old son Honorius as his co-ruler. Honorius had to be a fast learner, as Theo died less than two years later, leaving Honorius Emperor in the west at the age of 10. Seeing as he then oversaw the loss of his British provinces, and the Sack of Rome by the Visigoths, his apprenticeship doesn't seem to have done him much good.

HE WANTS TO CALL IT *WHAT?*

Imagine you're a national icon, a war hero, an inspiration to all (it's hard, Dads, but give it a go). You decide that what the country needs is a new organisation to give young lads leadership and inculcate in them patriotism, chivalry and good old British fair play. You've even come up with a title: *Scouting for Boys.*
You probably wouldn't get that idea off the ground now, but on this day in 1908 Robert Baden-Powell published the first volume of his scoutcraft book and set the ball rolling on a youth movement that by 2010 encompassed over 32 million Boy Scouts worldwide, giving Dads approximately 64 million hours of free time every week.

HERE COMES THE BRIDE

Mendelssohn's famous 'Wedding March' from his music for *A Midsummer Night's Dream* is the traditional tune for married couples to walk out to after their nuptials (not to be confused with the 'Here Comes the Bride' music that she normally walks *in* to – that's Wagner's 'Bridal March' from *Lohengrin*). Mendelssohn's music was written in 1842, but it really took off in the public imagination when Queen Victoria's daughter (also called Victoria) married Prince Frederick William of Prussia on this day in 1858. And as it's the first tune he hears after passing on responsibility for his daughter to the groom, it's got a soft spot in the heart of Dads too.

SYDNEY WAS A RUM OLD COVE

Today is Australia Day, the date officially commemorating the British claiming possession of New South Wales in 1788. But the same day 20 years later was another important Aussie date, and one guaranteed to make Dads sit up and take notice, if only by its name. Some historians reckon the Rum Rebellion wasn't really about the crackdown on illicit booze at all; still, whatever its cause, the Governor of NSW had put a lot of noses out of joint and was deposed in an armed coup. His name was William Bligh, who had provoked the mutiny on the *Bounty* in 1789 – he was probably getting used to it …

WELCOME THE WIDGET

In the 1960s Guinness were working on a way to allow their customers to enjoy a similar product to draught beer in their own home. Their boffins filed a patent on this day in 1969 for a device inside the can that would discharge gas into the beer and give it that distinctive head. 'Technical problems' meant the project was put on hold, and it wasn't until the 1980s that Guinness returned to the challenge. After rejecting dozens of methods, they finally launched the nitrogen-dispensing widget at the end of the decade, and their competitors soon followed suit. And Dads ever since have been eternally grateful.

YUM-YUM!

Dads are pretty useless on dates (unless they end in '66, like 1066 or 1966), and not great at historical events in general. But there's one piece of history they've all heard of, although they haven't a clue when, where or what it was. It began today in 1521 and it was the DIET OF WORMS! And even though a 'Diet' was just an assembly and 'Worms' was (and still is) a city in Germany, Dads can't help finding it really funny. Don't tell them it was all about Martin Luther and the Protestant Reformation – they'd find it a real let-down.

NO LITTERING? NO PROBLEM!

Dads (and their kids) love snacking, but hate littering, so they're always wandering round with pockets full of empty wrappers trying to find a bin. The perfect treat for when you're on the move has got to be the ice-cream cone, and today in 1924 Carl Taylor received a patent for a cone-rolling machine. The invention complemented Ernest Hamwi's cone-*making* machine, patented four years earlier. Add the ice cream, and you have the ideal outdoor confection. Now, when are they going to invent a beer bottle made of pork scratchings?

TIT FOR TAT

30 Any Dad worth his salt will tell his kids that two wrongs don't make a right, but grown-ups never learn. On this day in 1649 Charles I of England was executed. And 12 years to the day later, following the Restoration of the monarchy, Oliver Cromwell's body was exhumed from Westminster Abbey and hung at Tyburn in a posthumous 'execution'. The head was put on a spike above Westminster Hall and stayed there for the next 24 years until a storm broke the pole it was on. Finally, after a long and tortuous journey through several owners, a head was solemnly buried at Sidney Sussex College (Cromwell's alma mater) in 1960, though whether it was the Lord Protector's is anyone's guess.

DO YOU WANT BORSCHT WITH THAT?

After centuries of subsisting on cabbage and vodka, Russian Dads finally had somewhere to take their offspring for a tasty meal on this day in 1990, when the first Moscow McDonald's opened. Twenty years later the Pushkin Square branch of the worldwide franchise was the busiest Golden Arches restaurant on the planet, serving some 40,000 customers every day. Although in 2014 Russian authorities closed down several branches for alleged 'sanitary reasons' (some people suspected it was more a result of US–Russian political tension), knowing Ronald McDonald it won't be long before he's dishing out the happy meals again.

FEBRUARY

WATCHING YOU WATCHING THEM

1 Big Brother arrived on this day in 1952 with the introduction of TV detector vans. The state-of-the-art vans would 'pass slowly along roads' picking up signals from TV sets, and detection officers would then call to check licences. The 'receiving licence' for radio signals was introduced in 1904, with 68 issued in the first two years. The TV licence arrived in 1946 and the vans, operated by the Post Office, were an attempt to track down the estimated 100,000 people watching without coughing up. Dads' favourite excuses include: 'I never watch the telly', 'I forgot to post it' and, of course, 'I thought my wife had done it'.

HE'S A BIG ONE

On 16 October 1869, two workers digging a well in Iowa discovered the petrified remains of a 3m (10ft) tall man; was it proof that giants had once walked the earth? Sadly, no. In a meticulous wind-up of which all Dads would be proud, tobacconist George Hull had bought a huge block of gypsum, hired a sculptor to produce a weathered 'giant' (and sworn him to secrecy), then buried it at his cousin's farm. A year later his cousin requested a well be dug in just the right spot and, hey presto! Soon they were charging 50 cents for a look at the giant. The public lapped it up, but not many scholars were fooled and the hoax was admitted in court today in 1870.

SAY CHEESE (1)

It's a red-letter day for all Dads devoted to dairy delights, for in 1815 the world's first commercial cheese factory opened in Switzerland. The inevitable (cheese) spread of industrial techniques in food production might have drastically reduced the variety on offer, but it does mean we can get our hands on a nice block of cheddar whenever we fancy. And for Dads who don't like cheese, here's a cheesy joke instead: What cheese is made backwards? Edam!

HAPPY BIRTHDAY, SIR NORMAN

Norman Wisdom was born into hardship today in 1915, but ended up an OBE and a knight of the realm. The hapless Norman Pitkin character he developed over several films was a huge hit, and he was the only Western actor whose films were allowed to be shown in Communist Albania, where the dictator Enver Hoxha was a fan. He was admittedly a bit of a Marmite character, particularly in his movies, but there's a certain type of Dad who can't resist that daft slapstick. Charlie Chaplin referred to him as 'my favourite clown', though, and that's good enough for me.

CHAMPAGNE FOR EVERYONE

Dads love the thought of a get-rich-quick scheme, so it was a great day for them in February 1922 when the first volume of *Reader's Digest* was published in the USA. By 1935 it was selling a million copies each month and three years later it launched in the UK. It was most famous for its Prize Draws, where millions of people would receive letters signed by the Prize Draw manager telling them they'd been 'specially selected' for the chance to win; for many years in the UK these were signed 'Tom Champagne' – and despite what you might think, it was his real name!

RAIN LATER

On this day in 1861 the foundations of a vital British tradition were laid when the first weather warning for shipping was broadcast by telegraph. It was the brainchild of Vice-Admiral Robert FitzRoy, who is the only person to have a shipping area named after them (in 2002, when the former area Finisterre needed renaming). Although most ships now rely on satellite data, the BBC shipping forecast is a much-loved institution listened to by many more people than actually need it. Countless Dads have rocked their infants to sleep in the small hours to its poetic cadence, preceded of course by the soothing strains of Ronald Binge's 'Sailing By'.

BYE-BYE BABY

The infamous dictator François 'Papa Doc' Duvalier gave Dads everywhere a bad name with his bloodthirsty regime that saw the murder of around 30,000 Haitians, and his son 'Baby Doc' wasn't much better when he took over in 1971 – he lived a life of luxury while his people starved. So it was a big hurray from Dads everywhere when Baby Doc was overthrown today in 1986 and forced to flee the country. Baby Doc returned in 2011 to 'help' his country but was arrested and in 2014 faced trial for corruption and human rights abuses.

WHAT THE DEVIL?

On this night in 1855 there was a heavy snowfall in Devon, to nobody's surprise. And when residents woke up the next morning, it seemed that someone – or something – had been out that night leaving a trail. Over a distance of between 60–160km (40–100 miles), a series of hoof-like trails had appeared. But what was perplexing was that the trails led straight over rivers, haystacks and houses, even being left on rooftops and high walls. Locals lost no time in blaming the devil for these cloven prints. Numerous theories have been put forward since, blaming runaway balloons, hopping rodents and escaped kangaroos, but whatever it was it seems too complicated and well executed to have been a Dad playing a trick on his kids.

HOW MUCH?

Dads are constantly amazed at the amount of money shelled out in football on transfer fees and wages, seemingly oblivious to the connection between this and their own willingness to stump up ever-increasing amounts for season tickets and Sky subscriptions. In August 2014 Manchester United smashed the British transfer record when they paid Real Madrid £59.7m for Ángel di Maria. But the most symbolic ceiling shattered was on this day in 1979, when Nottingham Forest paid Birmingham City £1.18m for Trevor Francis, making him Britain's first million-pound player and doubling the previous record paid just a month before. Francis repaid a huge chunk of that when he scored the winning goal for Forest in the European Cup final three months later.

TOM AND JERRY

Dads love slapstick cartoon violence, and nothing beats a bit of *Tom and Jerry*. The very first in the MGM series, *Puss Gets the Boot*, was released today in 1940, and another 113 were to follow up until 1957, winning seven Oscars for best animated short film and showcasing the talents of William Hanna and Joseph Barbera to the world. In this first cartoon, Tom is called Jasper and Jerry is Jinx (though the mouse's name isn't mentioned) – for the follow-up (*The Midnight Snack*) animator John Carr won $50 for suggesting the names Tom and Jerry, and the rest is cartoon history.

DUCK! NO, QUAIL!

Be honest, if you were told a Vice-President of the USA had shot his companion rather than the game on a hunting trip, Quayle would be the first name that sprang to mind. And quail does feature in this story, being the one that got away. On this day in 2006 Dick Cheney was out shooting with attorney Harry Whittington when he took a pot-shot at a bird and instead hit Harry, peppering him with lead. A few days later Harry emerged from hospital and actually apologised to the Veep 'for all that he had been through'! It's the sort of misunderstanding any Dad can empathise with.

WHY DON'T WE HEAD EAST INSTEAD?

Although they tend to calm down a bit once they've got kids to think about, some Dads have a bit of a boy-racer past, and dream of whizzing along with the wind in their hair on some daring exploit. The 1908 New York–Paris Race, which began today, would have been right up their street. Hang on, though. New York to Paris? Surely that's just a jaunt across the Atlantic? Well, yes, but these chaps went the other way round the world, calling at Vladivostok, Moscow and Berlin on the way. Three out of six entrants finished, and the winner arrived in Paris on 30 July.

LET THERE BE LIGHT!

The aptly named Lumière brothers, Auguste and Louis, were pioneers of motion pictures in late 19th-century France. Their *cinématographe* was patented today in 1895 and in December they held the first public screening of films at which admission was charged. But rather than go on to dominate film-making, they declared, 'cinema is an invention without any future', and the far-sighted brothers moved on to developing colour photography. Fortunately others stepped in to ensure we didn't miss out on such classics as Eddie Murphy's *Daddy Day Care* (2003), Fred Astaire's *Daddy Long Legs* (1955) and Jack Lemmon's *Dad* (1989).

VALENTINE

St Valentine was a third-century Roman saint who came to a sticky end (beaten nearly to death and beheaded, since you ask) – Geoffrey Chaucer first linked him to the idea of romantic love in his poem 'The Parliament of Birds'. But why should today make you proud to be a Dad? Surely romance flies out of the window once the nappies start piling up? Well, that's the point. Dads who (pre-fatherhood) either forgot Valentine's Day or couldn't see the point in it now have an excuse – 'I was worrying so much about little Charlie/Charlotte, love, it went clean out of my head.'

DECIMAL DAY

Although Dads can be traditional types stuck in the past, it must be admitted that trying to calculate money in pounds, shillings and pence could be a bit of a bind – 4 farthings in a penny, 12 pennies in a shilling, 20 shillings in a pound ... So although it was a bit of a wrench to say farewell to the florin, the half-crown and the good old threepenny bit, when the UK went decimal today in 1971 it did make it easier to add things up. And it gave Arkwright-type grocers the opportunity to p-p-put their p-p-prices up a bit at the same time!

THAT'S WHY I FORGET THINGS

Great news for Dads on this day in 2008 with the publication of an article in *New Scientist* called 'Forgetfulness is Key to a Healthy Mind'. In it, Jessica Marshall highlighted the case of a woman referred to as 'AJ' who could never forget anything. In a case of what was dubbed 'hyperthymestic syndrome', poor old AJ could remember tiny details of her daily life going back years – and it was driving her nuts! It turns out that it's vital to have the ability to forget things in order to stay sane and to free up space for useful memories – so a Dad's highly developed capacity to forget everyday stuff is a jolly good thing.

WHAT DO I DO FOR THE NEXT
299 YEARS, 346 DAYS?

17 Dads are obsessed with the weather: will it be dry enough to mow the lawn? Will the cricket be washed out? Have I got to put antifreeze in the car yet? So the launch of the first weather satellite, Vanguard 2, today in 1959 was great news. The 50cm (20in) diameter magnesium sphere was designed to monitor and transmit data on cloud cover for 19 days using its mercury batteries. After that, its drag was designed to be monitored from the ground to provide information on atmospheric density for the lifetime of its orbit … estimated to be about 300 years.

🚭 MILKING ON BOARD

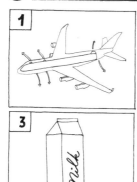

LOOK OUT!

18

There's an old Dad ditty that goes: 'As I sat under the apple tree a birdie sent his love to me/And as I wiped it from my eye/I said, "Thank goodness cows can't fly!"' But watch out ... on this day in 1930 Elm Farm Ollie did just that. Granted, the Guernsey was in a plane flying from Bismarck, Missouri, to St Louis, but she not only became the world's first flying cow, but the first to be milked in-flight. The milk was then sealed in paper cartons and parachuted to people on the ground. It was probably milkshake by the time it arrived ...

'AND I LOVE HAIR ...'

19 Wigs, toupees, hairpieces ... call them what you will, but as a Dad's hairiness seems to be in inverse proportion to how many kids he has, there was a time when these handy contraptions were *de rigueur* for balding fathers. False hair was very big in the 1960s, which makes you wonder how Brits could spare the *half-ton* of Beatles wigs we shipped to the USA on this day in 1964, 10 days after the Fab Four's landmark appearance on *The Ed Sullivan Show*.

FIFTY UP, LOOK YOU

20 You could be forgiven for thinking that most of this book has been compiled from the pages of Uncyclopedia, the Internet's antidote to Wikipedia, but you'd be mistaken. There are far too many correct facts in this book to have come from the site that Wikipedia describes as 'a satirical website that parodies Wikipedia'. Uncyclopedia, which is a booby trap for careless Dads 'helping' with homework, in turn informs us that Wikipedia was originally written entirely in Klingon. Seems possible. Today in 2008 the 50th language was added to Uncyclopedia – Welsh. And we learn from its august pages that when the Romans left Wales, they took several things with them, including 'almost all of the vowels'.

STEAMING TO SUCCESS

Dads are suckers for a steam train (see 19 April), and what a sight it must have been today in 1804 when Richard Trevithick's locomotive pulled a train along a tramway at a Welsh ironworks for the first time. The Cornishman had been dabbling in steam since his days at the wonderfully named Ding Dong Mine near Penzance (mainly to avoid having to pay fellow pioneers Boulton and Watt royalties for their steam pumps), but he had to overcome setbacks such as exploding boilers. When his unnamed loco successfully hauled 10 tons of iron at Merthyr, he also won a wager for the works owner.

A GOOD DAY FOR HARES

Hare coursing is not a particularly nice pastime, especially for the hares. In 1912 Owen Smith had the idea of using an artificial hare, intending to remove the cruelty and put greyhound racing on a par with horse racing. Eight years later the first mechanical hare was used at the first professional greyhound track, in Emeryville, California, today in 1920. The innovation became very popular in the UK: by 1946 it had 34 million paying spectators, mainly because it was somewhere people could place a bet. And Dads love a bit of a flutter (see 24 May).

THIRD TIME LUCKY

Dads are used to the odd narrow escape, but the experience of John 'Babbacombe' Lee in 1885 was cutting things fine. Convicted of murder, and protesting his innocence, Lee was due to hang on this day at Exeter Prison. Three times the lever was pulled, and each time the trapdoor failed to open. As a result his sentence was commuted to life imprisonment and he was released in 1907. Later investigations showed his let-off was mechanically rather than divinely inspired: the trapdoor when weighted rested on 3mm of a drawbar, just enough to stop it opening.

WHERE ARE MY SCISSORS?

Let's face it, neatness isn't the strength of most Dads. And in the early days of postage stamps, each stamp on a sheet had to be cut individually. Fortunately, Henry Archer invented a machine to put perforations into stamp sheets, and by 1854 all UK postage stamps were perforated. On this day in 1857 our American cousins caught up and the 3-cent George Washington became the first perforated US stamp. Stamps commonly have between 11 and 14 holes between each one, which still didn't stop careless Dads ripping them in pieces until the recent introduction of ready-separated self-adhesive stamps.

GIVE ME SHELTER

Dads in the run-up to World War Two were given something to tinker with in their gardens from today in 1939 when the first Anderson shelter was installed in Islington, London. Named after Sir John Anderson, in charge of civil defence, they were basically curved sheets of corrugated iron sunk half into the ground and covered with earth – not much use for a direct hit but good enough for blast protection. Many Dads grew vegetables on top of their shelters, prompting one wag to observe, 'There is more danger of being hit by a vegetable marrow falling off the roof ... than of being hit by a bomb!'

IT'S NOT A RACE, IT'S A LOTTERY ...

... is a criticism that has been levelled at Dads' favourite horse race, the Grand National. So it's quite appropriate that the winner of the first properly organised Grand Liverpool Steeplechase on this day in 1839 was called Lottery. The contest received its 'National' moniker in 1847. There were 17 runners in the first race, seven of whom fell, including one ridden by Captain Martin Becher, who fell at the first brook, remounted and promptly fell again at the second brook, which is a rather damp way of getting a fence named after you ...

IT'S JUST NOT CRICKET (1)

27 Upper lips must have quivered on this day in 1874 when the first game of baseball to be played in England took place at Kennington Oval cricket ground, of all places. The game was a precursor to a tour of England by teams from Boston and Philadelphia later in the year. Baseball became quite popular for a time (witness Derby County FC's old ground being known as the Baseball Ground), with its peak of popularity coming in the 1930s when crowds of up to 10,000 attended games. And the good news for Dads – it never quite caught on, and cricket retained its place as *the* summer sport.

SABBATH SNOOZE

28 Not so many Dads are familiar with the inside of a house of worship in these godless times, but those who are would sympathise with Roger Scott, who on this day in 1643 in Swampscott, Massachusetts, was in court charged with sleeping in church. Described as 'that drowsy sinner', poor old Roger ended up being whipped – although that might have been as much for thumping the person who woke him up! It's all reminiscent of the Dad who complained that the service was too long and his bottom had gone to sleep. 'I know,' said Mum, 'I heard it snoring!'

MARCH

IS THERE ANY BODY THERE?

On Christmas Day 1977 Charlie Chaplin died and was buried in Switzerland. Then on 1 March 1978 two unemployed car mechanics dug him up, purloined his body and demanded a ransom from the family. Charlie's widow Oona very sensibly ignored them, saying, 'My husband is in heaven and in my heart,' and the amateurish 'kidnappers' were caught 11 weeks later and the body recovered, buried in a picturesque spot in a cornfield. It was so pretty Oona is said to have remarked, 'In a way it's a shame that we found him!' Charlie's son Eugene could see the funny side of his Dad's disappearance 25 years on – in 2014 he had a small part in *The Price of Fame*, a comedy based on the incident.

BON VOYAGE

On this day in 1982, ITV viewers settled down to watch the latest adaptation of John Mortimer's autobiographical play *A Voyage Round My Father*. Starting life as a series of radio programmes in 1963, it became a 1969 TV play, then a 1970s stage play before this BAFTA-winning version appeared, starring Alan Bates as Mortimer and Laurence Olivier as his father, around whom the play revolves. Witty and perceptive, it explores the father-son relationship with Mortimer's customary skill.

WHAT, NO CHIPS?

On this day in 1939 a peculiar craze began that set US colleges alight for a couple of months before (thank goodness) fizzling out. To win a $10 bet, Harvard student Lothrop Withington Jr swallowed a live goldfish. Like 2014's Ice Bucket Challenge with indigestion (but without the charity), before you could say 'fish' it seemed every student in the States was at it: one chap swallowed 87! The sentiments of Dads across America was probably summed up in this ditty published in the *Boston Herald*: 'To end this paranoiac prank/ Oh Harvard, how I wish/ You'd put the students in a tank/ And graduate the fish!'

WALKING INTO HISTORY

Many Dads have made stupid bets and regretted it when they lost them. The American Edward Payson Weston wagered a friend on the outcome of the 1860 Presidential election – whichever's candidate lost would walk the 769km (478 miles) from Boston to Washington to see the inauguration. When Abraham Lincoln won, Weston kept his promise, leaving Boston on 22 February 1861 and arriving 10 days later on 4 March. It gave him a taste for long-distance walking, and he is credited with the great popularity of competitive walking as a sport in the late 19th century. His incredible story was told in fascinating detail in *A Man in a Hurry* (deCoubertin Books, 2012).

SPITFIRE DEBUT

Many Dads will have patiently glued together Airfix Spitfires in their youth, but the first flight of the real thing was on this day in 1936, when Captain Joseph Summers took R.J. Mitchell's new design up for an eight-minute flight from Eastlcigh aerodrome near Southampton. The plane that pilots loved to fly went on to save the country (along with the Hurricane) in the Battle of Britain, and 20,351 were made at a cost of around £10,000 each before production finished in 1948. It was the only British fighter aircraft to be in continuous production before, during and after World War Two.

NOTHING ACTS FASTER THAN ACETYLSALICYLIC ACID

Dads can't keep track of what's good for them and what isn't, but doctors seem agreed (for now at least) that an aspirin a day does more than cure your headache; it has been advanced as reducing the incidence of heart attack and stroke, and the latest suggestion is that it can help prevent some cancers. Regular use does increase the risk of internal bleeding, so you should always ask your doctor before starting to take aspirin as a preventive, but it does seem to be an increasingly nifty little tablet. And the brand name 'Aspirin' was registered by drug company Bayer today in 1899 at the Imperial Patent Office in Berlin.

DINOSAURS ALIVE AND WELL IN OHIO

Or they were in 1908, when the mayor of Cincinnati, Leopold Markbreit, declared that 'women are not physically fit to operate automobiles'. Let's concede that in those early days it might have taken more physical effort to drive a vehicle, but it's still something you can't imagine even Jeremy Clarkson saying today. Dads today are much more appreciative of female capabilities (particularly their capability to launch a well-aimed projectile at anyone making stupid sexist comments). Markbreit died the following year; history does not record if he was run over by an irate lady motorist.

EXPENSIVE BABE

 Dads love it when someone else is proved spectacularly wrong. On this day in 1930 baseball legend Babe Ruth signed a two-year deal with the New York Yankees worth $80,000 a year. When he was asked to justify earning $5,000 more than President Herbert Hoover, Ruth pointed out, 'I had a better year than Hoover,' which seems fair enough. Of more interest to us are the words of Yankees executive Ed Barrow, who insisted, 'No one will *ever* be paid more than Ruth.' In 2013 the Yankees' third baseman, Alex Rodriguez, was paid $29,000,000 – or as near as damn it $80,000 *per day*.

AT LAST - A DIET I CAN STICK TO!

On this day in 2011 a certain J. Wilson modified his diet to cut out one or two food groups, in fact everything except water and – wait for it, Dads – beer. Starting on the first day of Lent, the 38-year-old sought to emulate the monks of 16th-century Germany who fasted up until Easter and survived on *doppelbock* beer – 'liquid bread'. He joined forces with an Iowa brewery to come up with an especially nutritious beer, Illuminator Doppelbock, of which he drank four to five bottles a day for 46 days. And the result? The already skinny Wilson lost a further 11kg (25lb) during Lent!

STAND UP AND BE COUNTED

It's easy for Dads to lose count of all the kids in their house: has the eldest really moved out? He seems to have a lot of meals here ... What we need is a proper census, and today in 1801 we got one, the first official census since William the Conqueror, and they've been held every 10 years since (except in 1941 during World War Two). They're normally pretty accurate, although apparently Scottish football legend Matt Busby confused the enumerator with his heavy accent in 1931 when he was playing for Manchester City. Legend has it that under 'Occupation' he was entered as a 'fruit boiler'!

COURANT AFFAIRS

On this day in 1702 Dads finally had something to read with their morning tea and toast when the first regular daily newspaper, the *Daily Courant*, was published by Elizabeth Mallet in premises near the Fleet Bridge. It was a single sheet with largely foreign news on the front, adverts on the back and no comment; Mallet believed that her readers had 'sense enough to make reflections for themselves', so she'd have been useless as a modern tabloid publisher. In 1735 the *Courant* disappeared when it was merged with the *Daily Gazetteer*.

BLESS ME, FATHER ... OR MOTHER

Samuel Johnson was once said to have compared a woman preaching to a dog walking on two legs: 'It is not done well; but you are surprised to find it done at all.' Outrageous sexism from the great lexicographer there, who would not have been pleased today in 1994 at the ordination of the first 32 female Anglican priests at Bristol Cathedral. Modern Dads, however, would be very comfortable with the idea of being married to one: after all, they wouldn't have to pass comment on whether black was 'her colour' or whether her bum 'looked big in this cassock'.

DAD'S DECORATING DISASTER

On this day in 1915 the music-hall entertainer Billy Williams – aka the Man in the Velvet Suit – died aged just 37. Born in Australia, his stage career led him to England in 1899, where he lived until his death. He made over 500 recordings, mainly of comic songs, the most popular and long-lived of which was Weston and Barnes' classic 'When Father Papered the Parlour', a cautionary tale for Dads everywhere. With Mum 'stuck to the ceiling' and the kids 'stuck to the floor', it was no wonder that 'you couldn't see Pa for paste'. Some things never change …

BANG GOES BYNG

Dads can take heart from knowing that however much they let down their family, they won't suffer the fate that Admiral John Byng did today in 1757. The Articles of War had been changed in 1749 to make senior officers subject to the same discipline as other ranks. This was bad timing for the hapless admiral who, in 1756, chose not to pursue a French fleet off Menorca with his damaged vessels, a decision that ultimately cost Britain possession of the island. There was public uproar and when Byng was court-martialled for failing to 'do his utmost', the new inflexible code meant he had to be shot.

CRICKET STANDS THE TEST OF TIME

Dads love a good coincidence, seeing them as being full of hidden meaning. Well, today in 1877 an Australian XI lined up against their English counterparts at Melbourne Cricket Ground for a two-innings match that would retrospectively be seen as the first example of the classic form of a classic sport – Test cricket. It wasn't known as the Ashes at the time – that would have to wait until 1882/3 – but was nevertheless keenly fought, with Australia winning by 45 runs. One hundred years later, the Centenary Test was played at the same ground between the same opponents. Australia won again – by 45 runs.

THAT REMINDS ME ...

Dads are famous for not having a round tuit, stopping them from doing all sorts of things: 'I'll put that shelf up when I get a round tuit ... I'll fill that form in when I get a round tuit.' (Good news: they're now available online.) But what the state of Mississippi did today in 1995 made Dads feel better about their lack of get-up-and-go – they finally ratified the 13th Amendment to the Constitution from 1865. You know, the little one about abolishing slavery ... To cap it off, they then forgot to send their ratification to the US Archivist to make it official until 2013!

I'M STARTING A NEW BAND

Whether it's holding together some household appliance instead of replacing it or doing a proper repair, wrapped around his finger to remind him to do something (although he forgets what), or just being flipped ambitiously at a fly on the wall, the humble rubber band has myriad uses for your typical Dad. And it was patented today in England in 1845 by Stephen Perry. It's a handy alternative to a money clip too (if you've got any) – drugs baron Pablo Escobar apparently spent $2,500 every month on rubber bands to keep his illicit cash tidy.

DAD PLEADS MITTY-GATION

When a James Thurber story appeared in *New Yorker* magazine on this day in 1938, few probably guessed he had created a character that would fire the public imagination to the extent that his name would end up in the *Oxford English Dictionary*. The hapless, henpecked Walter Mitty imagined himself flying planes, carrying out surgical operations and phlegmatically facing a firing squad. And what Dad hasn't had Mitty-ish daydreams of his own? The ceiling he is painting becomes the Sistine Chapel; the lawn he is mowing is Wembley Stadium; and as he struggles to remember his computer password, he is cracking the Engima code itself …

'AVE A SWISSKIT? - NO, AVALANCHE!

One of Dads' favourite 1970s telly ads involved the intrepid 'I'll risk it for a Swisskit' man cheerfully surviving a snowslip. And there was a real-life survival story after an avalanche today in 1775 completely buried a farm and barn in the Italian Alps. It seemed clear all four occupants must have perished, so no rescue attempt was made. When the thaw set in 37 days later locals went to recover the bodies and instead found three survivors – they'd been trapped in the barn and had survived on goats' milk. It's the longest anyone has ever survived being trapped by an avalanche.

I'LL JUST CALL IT EYJA ...

Dads love the peace and quiet of their garden, but spare a thought for anyone living under a flight path nowadays. So when the volcano Eyjafjallajökull in Iceland first gave a little hiccup today in 2010, it was a sign of good news on the way for the Noise Abatement Society. Less than a month later it threw up a massive ash cloud that led to the closure of European airspace from 15–20 April, the largest disruption of commercial air traffic since World War Two. And though thousands of passengers were left stranded, and millions had to cancel plans, for Dads enjoying an unexpectedly silent sky it seemed a small price to pay.

DADS' NAVY

In early 1942 the USA had just entered World War Two and were looking to supply Allied forces in the Pacific. Most Australian military vessels and troops were already fully committed. So on this day Mission X was conceived by General MacArthur when he arrived in Melbourne to coordinate strategy. What became known as the 'Ragtag Fleet' was in effect a maritime Dads' Army, comprising 3,327 Aussies either too young, old or 'unfit' for military service who wanted to do their bit. And for the next three and a half years they provided support to the Allies on New Guinea, the Philippines and beyond, ferrying in vital supplies and equipment, often under enemy fire.

HUGO, THE AMAZING ESCABIBLIOGIST?

Hugo de Groot (1583–1645) was a jurist, theologian, philosopher, historian, poet, diplomat and playwright. In short, he was just the kind of Renaissance smart alec know-it-all your average Dad would take an instant dislike to. However, Hugo did one exciting thing in his life. Sentenced to life imprisonment in a Dutch castle for his unconventional religious views, today in 1621 he daringly escaped hidden in a book chest. The chest he hid in is now on display either in Amsterdam or Delft, depending on which one you believe has the original!

LADY KITTY LOSES BATTLE
TO SEE MATCH

Dads who are naturally suspicious of satnavs ('Don't tell *me* which way to go') were vindicated on this day in 2008 when a taxi arrived to drive Lady Kitty Spencer and a friend the 137km (85 miles) from the Spencer Estate at Althorp, Northamptonshire, to Chelsea's home ground in London for a match with Arsenal. The driver punched 'Stamford Bridge' into the satnav, followed the instructions and, some time later, duly arrived at the historic Yorkshire village where King Harold defeated Harold Hardrada in 1066, a mere 370km (230 miles) away from where the football game was kicking off. Never mind, think of the money she saved on Bovril …

I'D LIKE TO THANK MY DAD ...
AND I'D LIKE TO THANK MY SON

Sons have a lot to thank their Dads for, but one returned the compliment in style in 1948. Film director and screenwriter John Huston cast his own father, Walter, as an old-time gold prospector in *The Treasure of the Sierra Madre*, a gripping tale of greed and treachery. And today in 1949, Walter won Best Supporting Actor at the Oscars ceremony. His son trumped him though, winning Best Director and Best Adapted Screenplay for the same film. It was the first time a father and son had won Oscars. Incredibly, in the 1980s John Huston directed his daughter Angelica in an Oscar-winning performance for *Prizzi's Honor*.

CAMBRIDGE GET THE BLUES

The last time most Dads enjoyed watching the University Boat race was on this day in 1978, and for one very simple reason – the Boat Race is only worth bothering with when somebody sinks. What could be better than watching nine of our country's elite students floundering around in the cold spring waters of the Thames from the comfort of your armchair? Well, how about watching 18 elite students floundering around, etc., etc.? What a pity there was no telly in 1912, when both boats sank!

I THINK I'VE JUST WORKED OUT WHAT'S CAUSING IT!

Don't get me wrong – it's great being a Dad, and this book is a celebration of it. But you can have too much of a good thing. William and Elizabeth Greenhill had 39 children in the late 17th century (all but seven of them girls, and all single births except one set of twins). That's a heck of a lot of nappies! So it was fantastic news today in 1918 when family planning took a huge leap forward with the publication of Marie Stopes' *Married Love*, meaning Mums and Dads could finally take control of the size of their brood.

RISING TO THE CHALLENGE

While we're on the subject, we might as well tackle the delicate topic of bedroom relations. Knowing how embarrassed Dads are by such matters, I will skirt around the topic with maximum discretion. In the late 20th century, Pfizer research scientists looking into angina treatments synthesised the compound sildenafil and held clinical trials. It didn't have the intended effect, but it gave the male patients something to take their minds off their angina. And on this day in 1998, sildenafil was approved for medical use in the USA, and later that year began to be sold under its brand name – Viagra.

SWEET CAROLINE

Pirates, pop music and presidents – surely a combination no trendy Dad could resist. On this day in 1964 Radio Caroline, named after JFK's daughter, began broadcasting at noon when Simon Dee hit the airwaves. It was formed by Irish businessman Ronan O'Rahilly to circumvent the stranglehold the BBC had on traditional broadcasting in the UK – by transmitting from a ship in international waters the authorities at first could do nothing to stop him. With a disregard for the facts any Dad would be proud of, despite broadcasting on a frequency of 197.3 they plugged themselves poetically as 'Caroline on 199'!

I'LL DO IT ... NEXT YEAR

The London Marathon has become a fixture on the international marathon circuit since the inaugural race on this day in 1981. Just over 7,700 runners started and 6,255 of those finished the course – in 2014 there were around 36,000 entrants, many raising money for their favourite charity and hundreds making it harder for themselves by running in fancy dress. The event grabbed the public's attention from the start, especially when the first contest was won jointly by Dick Beardsley and Inge Simonsen, who sportingly chose to cross the line together rather than race it out. And every year Dads watch it and say the same thing: 'Next year ...'

JUST WHAT I NEEDED

Hats off to Hymen L. Lipman of Philadelphia, an inspiration to Dads everywhere. To begin with, on this day in 1858 he was granted a patent for being the first person to think of sticking a little rubber on the end of pencils – after all, even Dads make mistakes occasionally. Secondly, he sold the patent for $100,000 four years later. Finally, in 1875 the US Supreme Court ruled the patent invalid and worthless: 'What you've basically done,' they said, 'is stick one invention on top of another.' Which you'd have thought would have been patently obvious 17 years earlier, really.

AND THE AWARD FOR BEST AWARDS CEREMONY GOES TO ...

... The Razzies! Dads hate awards ceremonies (probably the only things they 'win' are those mass-produced 'World's Greatest Dad' mugs), but let's make an exception for the Golden Raspberry Awards, accolades handed out to recognise the very worst movies of the year. The first was an informal affair in the living room of copywriter John Wilson today in 1981 in front of three dozen people, but now it's a well-attended bash. Not many award-winners turn up to get their prize, so congratulations to Halle Berry and Sandra Bullock, both of whom have collected their Worst Actress awards in person.

APRIL

OLAF LIRPO STRIKES AGAIN

1 Yes, that famous Finn and his friends Paolo Fril and Flora Poli have been inspiring Dads since time immemorial to play 'hilarious' tricks on their kids. No one can be certain of the origins of the April Fool custom, but it's now honoured mainly in the media. The most famous is probably still *Panorama*'s 'spaghetti harvest' spoof from 1957, but one of the cleverest was the *Guardian*'s seven-page supplement in 1977 on the idyllic holiday destination San Serriffe, comprising two islands (Upper Caisse and Lower Caisse) that just happened to be shaped like a semicolon.

WHY NO CHICKEN CROSSING?

With the plethora of animal-themed traffic crossings, you'd have thought the chicken, butt of so many road-related Dad jokes, would have been included. We'd had the good old-fashioned zebra crossing in Britain since 1949, but today in 1962 technology began its jack-booted march when the first panda crossing was unveiled in London. With its confusing combination of 'flashing' and 'pulsating' amber lights, the endangered panda was soon superseded by pelicans, puffins and toucans. Since 2007 there have even been equestrian Pegasus crossings – though any creature less in need of help crossing the road than a winged horse is hard to imagine …

IT'S A BIT COLD UP HERE

The 14th Duke of Hamilton was a real Boys' Own hero and a great role model for Dads to inspire their kids with. He was an early flying pioneer, the youngest squadron leader of his day, and was the chap German deputy PM Rudolf Hess surrendered to in World War Two. Not only that, he was humble enough to work at the coalface of his father's mines to experience what it was like for the miners. He was also a sensible fellow, taking the easy way up Everest on this day in 1933 when he became the first person to fly over the world's highest mountain.

I'LL DO IT IN A MINUTE

Dads in need of an excuse not to rush into anything were given the perfect example today in 1581, when Francis Drake was knighted on board the *Golden Hind* by Elizabeth I for filling her treasury with Spanish loot. Granted, this was seven years before he insisted on finishing his game of bowls before fighting the Armada, but his admirable prioritising of sport over work must surely have been a long-term trait. Mind you, the fact that he never actually became a father himself probably explains why this privateering, circumnavigating sea captain, mayor and MP got so much done!

FRAN-TASTIC!

On this day in 1971 Fran Phipps became the first woman to reach the North Pole when she accompanied her husband Welland, a pilot, who had gone to install a navigation beacon. Living for 10 years at Resolute in the Arctic Circle, however, Fran wasn't just along for the ride in anything she did, raising nine children and helping 'Weldy' run his arctic airline. When asked what the North Pole was like, she said, 'It looks like my back yard!' And, armed with this information, Dad needn't feel guilty about sending Mum to put the bins out in the middle of winter.

CAN I BACKDATE MINE TO THE 1990S?

This was a landmark day for new Dads in 2003 – the father of any child born from this day was eligible to two weeks' paternity leave. From April 2011 the scheme was extended so that partners of mothers who didn't use all their maternity allowance could add up to 26 weeks of the unused weeks to their leave. While the two weeks has proved popular, take-up of the extra time has been limited, probably due to the relatively low level of statutory paternity pay (and definitely nothing to do with Dad not wanting to be left on his own with a screaming baby …).

A BRIGHT SPARK

Up until the 1820s Dads found it tricky to get a real fire going, especially since there wouldn't be two boy scouts to rub together for another 80-odd years (see 24 January). So it was very useful today in 1827 when Stockton chemist John Walker sold his first 'Congreves' – friction matches. These wooden splinters, tipped with sulphide of antimony and chlorate of potash, were named after rocket pioneer William Congreve, and though the name didn't stick, the idea certainly did. Walker refused to patent his invention, so it could be available to all … what a considerate chap.

AINTREE PILE-UP

We've already touched on the soft spot Dads have for the Grand National (see 26 February). For a final word we have to go back to 1967, when an unprepossessing 100–1 shot named Foinavon was making stately progress at the back of the field. Then, at the 23rd fence, a loose horse veered across into the leader, and a domino effect ensued that completely blocked the fence. By the time Foinavon eventually arrived, there was just enough room for him to jump the hurdle, and he won by 20 lengths. In 1984 the barrier was named the Foinavon fence.

WAR 'EAR-O

If Dads had a 'favourite' historical war, it would probably be the one with the silliest name – the War of Jenkins' Ear. What was essentially a trade war with Spain began in 1739 and comprised a number of battles in which ... zzzz. OK, all you want to know is what happened to Jenkins. Robert Jenkins was captain of the merchant ship *Rebecca*, which was stopped by the Spanish in the Caribbean on this day in 1731 on suspicion of smuggling. The Spanish commander tied Jenkins to a mast, lopped his ear off and said to tell King George II he could expect the same treatment. The indignant reaction of Parliament on hearing of the insult ultimately led to war.

SHIRLEY SHOME MISHTAKE?

In 1960, the British Heavyweight Wrestling Championship was won on this day by Shirley Crabtree from Halifax. This wasn't some northern stereotype battleaxe with rollers in her hair who had climbed into the ring with a rolling pin, though ... Shirley was a bloke. Roll forward 15 years and Shirley had morphed into 'Big Daddy', star of the Saturday afternoon wrestling that was the main attraction of ITV's *World of Sport*. Starting off as a 'baddy', Big Daddy was so lovable that he ended up as a 'blue eye' – the not-so-gentle giant cheered on by everyone. He was so popular he even had a comic strip based on him in *Buster* in the early 1980s.

IT'LL NEVER CATCH ON (1)

Dads love having something to moan about, especially their kids' taste in music, so it was great when Bob Dylan broke onto the scene with his whiny, nasal vocal style and his tuneless harmonica. The frizzy-haired beatnik played his first big concert in New York today in 1961, opening for John Lee Hooker at Gerde's Folk City, and doubtless 16 years later those Dylan fans who now had kids of their own were passing opinions on the punk revolution – 'They can't sing and they can't play!'

APRIL

MICKEY LE MOUSE

12

What a great day when Disneyland Paris opened its doors today in 1992. Parsimonious Dads could now palm their kids off with a weekend in France instead of a fortnight in Florida, and to add to the fun the French got all hot under the collar at the extending Americanisation of their culture, with one journalist calling for Euro Disney to be burned down and a stage director dubbing it a 'cultural Chernobyl'. To cap (or beret?) it all, the expected full house on opening day failed to materialise because of – surprise, surprise – striking French transport workers.

HALLEY-LUJAH!

13

Dads get fed up of trying to point out interesting things to their kids only for them to gawp round saying, 'Where? I can't see it.' So it was good news today in AD 837 when Halley's Comet made its closest approach to Earth in recorded history, a mere 0.03 astronomical units away. If that sounds too close for comfort, and unmissable by even the doziest of ninth-century nippers, it was still 5.1 million km (3.2 million miles) from doing any damage. Astronomer Edmund Halley was the first person to predict the return of a comet, although the 76-year orbit meant he died before his calculations were proved more or less accurate.

LEFT, RIGHT, LEFT ... OH, PLEASE YOURSELVES

Today in 1831 an incident happened that highlighted the dangers of a) walking and b) not pleasing yourself – much safer for Dads to stay on the sofa. The Broughton suspension bridge was a fine structure only five years old, spanning the River Irwell near Manchester, yet it was no match for the 74 men of the 60th Rifle Corps. In the first recorded instance of mechanical resonance-related failure, the steady marching of the men set up a vibration that caused a bolt to snap and the bridge to collapse. No one was killed, but ever since then the British Army has ordered 'break step' when marching across a bridge.

SOMETHIN' STUPID

Dads are always looking for ways to bond with their daughters – they don't always want to go fishing and bog-snorkelling – and a great example was set on this day in 1967 when Frank Sinatra and daughter Nancy had a number one with their recording of C. Carson Parks' song 'Somethin' Stupid'. And if you don't think this is the best father–daughter single in recording history, its only competitor is Ozzy and Kelly Osbourne's 'Changes' (2003); also a number one, it was voted 27th worst single of the noughties in a feature by *Village Voice*.

'IT'S NOT JUST ME, THEN?'

Absent-minded Dads are always forgetting warnings or missing helpful signs. So it was a relief for any Boston Dad who sat in wet paint for the opening match of the 1946 baseball season against the Brooklyn Dodgers today that he wasn't alone and, for a change, it wasn't his fault; the cold weather had apparently prevented the newly painted seats from drying in time, but no one in charge realised until the complaints began pouring in. It cost the Boston Braves $6,000 in compensation.

WE LOVE ERNIE (1)

Imagine going to the bookies, placing a bet, your horse loses ... and you get your money back! It's every Dads' idea of heaven, which is probably why Premium Bonds have been so popular since they were introduced today in 1956 by Chancellor Harold Macmillan. The numbers are chosen by the Electronic Random Number Indicating Equipment, now in its fourth incarnation, and bond-holders can win anything from £25 to a cool million. The return on your investment might be statistically pretty poor, but the chance of hitting the jackpot while being able to get your hands on your original cash still makes it too good to miss for millions of us.

HERE IS THE NEWS ... ERR ...

It might seem hard to believe now that the BBC bombards us with 24-hour non-stop news, most of it bad, but it seems there was a time when dear old 'Auntie' only told the listener what had actually happened, instead of what they thought was going to happen plus what has happened 50, 70, 100 years ago etc. Dads have got enough to worry about without hearing about the world's troubles, so it was an oasis of calm today in 1930 when the BBC announced that there had been no news that day and played some piano music instead.

THOMAS MAKES PEOPLE CHUFFED

Dads nowadays are not ashamed to read bedtime stories to their kids, thank goodness. And the adventures of *Thomas the Tank Engine* and his friends are as popular as ever. The first stories, devised by the Reverend Wilbert Awdry to entertain his son Christopher during a bout of measles, were published in 1945 and he finally put down his pen in 1972 with the publication of the 26th book, *Tramway Engines*. On this day in 2009 the *Independent on Sunday* included Thomas in their 'Happy List', a collection of 100 things that make Britain 'a happier place to live'.

GONE IN A FLASH

Dads love a bit of cheekiness, and what could be cheekier than a streaker? The first recorded streaker was arrested in London in 1799 after a chap accepted a 10-guinea bet (obviously) to run naked from Cornhill to Cheapside. The trend took off in the 1970s, however, and the first streaker at a major sporting event was Michael O'Brien, who interrupted a rugby international at Twickenham wearing his birthday suit on this day in 1974. The photo of his modesty being preserved by a strategically placed policeman's helmet became famous, and the helmet is now on display in the Twickenham Museum.

TO BOLDLY GO WHERE NO CAN HAS GONE BEFORE

Dads of all ages have grown up with *Star Trek* in one form or another, and creator Gene Roddenberry finally achieved his ambition to go into space when a few grams of his ashes were sent into orbit in a canister on a Celestis spacecraft today in 1997. The craft's orbit steadily declined and burned up on re-entering Earth's atmosphere on 20 May 2002. In 2016 more of Roddenberry's ashes will blast off on a mission to launch them into deep space. Let's 'cling on' to the hope that they one day are found by alien life.

DIY? IT'S ALL GREEK TO ME!

22

In 2010 the *Daily Telegraph* reported on the discovery of what might have been the first IKEA-style build-it-yourself instructions in the Apennine Mountains near the city of Potenza, southern Italy. When archaeologists discovered a sixth-century, Greek-style temple they found that nearly every surviving part was inscribed with instructions detailing how it should be put together. It's thought that when the local nobs developed a taste for Greek architecture, an Iron Age Del Boy decided to fill a gap in the market by supplying them with cheap self-assembly versions. Whether the Italian Dads that erected it ever bothered to read the instructions is another matter …

BY GEORGE!

It's St George's Day, and among other things that means the monarch will announce any new names to the Order of the Garter, the most ancient and noble order of chivalry in the UK. Membership is limited to 24 Companions at any time, and is by invitation of the monarch only, so any common-or-garden Dads thinking it would suit them down to the ground might be disappointed. Dating back to the 14th century, the order was founded by Edward III, who dished out the first honours on this day in 1344. Its motto is *Honi soit qui mal y pense*, or 'Evil to Him Who Evil Thinks'.

MONKEY BUSINESS

The first ever trial to be broadcast live on American radio was that of teacher John Scopes, who was charged that on this day in 1925 he had taught the theory of evolution to a class of high-school children and thus broken Tennessee's recently passed Butler Act. Scopes had invited the charge by encouraging his students to testify against him – the American Civil Liberties Union was looking for a test case to show up the unreasonableness of the law. Scopes was convicted, the law was discredited, and Dads discovered why they spent so much time lounging about all day picking their noses.

I THINK WE'LL TRY MARS THIS YEAR

One-upmanship Dads are always looking for somewhere new to take the family on holiday, so it probably won't be too long before you can't move in outer space for squabbling kids ('It's *my* turn to do a space walk!') and harassed parents ('I thought *you'd* shut the air lock?') ticking off their bucket lists ('Black hole? Check. Exploding supernova? Check.'). And it will all be the fault of people like multimillionaire Mark Shuttleworth, who today in 2002 became only the second-ever space tourist when he paid $20m for a seat in a Russian rocket to the International Space Station.

NO BIRTHDAY SUITS, PLEASE!

It's every Dad's worst nightmare. There you are, strolling in the Swiss Alps with your family, when you turn a corner and walk slap-bang into a party of Germans with their Bratwurst on display for all to see. Well, no longer after this day in 2009, when the sensible citizens of Appenzell Inner Rhodes voted by a show of hands to ban rambling in the altogether, which had become an increasingly popular pastime for German visitors to their canton. From this day tourists in their birthday suits would be fined 200 Swiss francs. And serve them right.

WHAT'S IT LIKE BEING A GUINEA PIG?

It's hard to imagine nowadays how worrying even the simplest childhood infections could be in the days before antibiotics. Today in 1944 Horton Corwin Hinshaw and William Feldman began testing streptomycin against tuberculosis in Minnesota. What they needed for their research were some guinea pigs, so they decided to use … guinea pigs! The poor little things were deliberately infected with TB, but five days after having the new antibiotic they were cured, and a few months later the new drug was being used successfully on humans.

MARVELLOUS MARVIN

In 1978 the wonderful *Hitchhikers' Guide to the Galaxy* debuted on British radio, the first of many formats for Douglas Adams' unique take on life, the universe and everything. One of the most popular characters in it was a depressed little fellow all us Dads can identify with: Marvin ('brain the size of a planet') the Paranoid Android. Voiced by Stephen Moore on radio and TV, when *Hitchhikers'* hit the big screen today in 2005 it was Alan Rickman who got to deliver such Marvinisms as, 'I have a million ideas but they all point to certain death.'

74

BALLOON BALLS-UP

It must have seemed like a great way for NASA to launch a multi-million-dollar space telescope – send up a huge helium balloon from the Australian outback. But, as Dads can testify, balloons have a nasty habit of blowing up in your face, and so it proved today in 2010. High winds caught the canopy and sent the expensive payload careering along the ground, smashing up cars (and itself) and sending onlookers running for their lives. 'We have learned a lot from this incident,' said one of the launch directors. Maybe Dad could try that excuse next time he makes a complete mess of something …

I CANNOT TELL A LIE

George Washington reached the political heights today in 1789 when he was sworn in as the first President of the USA. As all good Dads tell their kids, it was proof that telling the truth is always the right thing. Good little George confessed to his father that he'd chopped down the prize cherry tree, was forgiven for his honesty, and went on to liberate and govern his country. Whether modern-day Dads would be quite so forgiving if Junior admitted dropping the iPad on the patio or shaving rude words into the dog's fur is a moot point.

MAY

SPENDING A PENNY

Getting caught short in public is embarrassing, and many a Dad has had to find a discreet hedge for his offspring or a secluded corner to place a potty. But on this day in 1851 London's Great Exhibition began, and part of the attraction was George Jennings' Monkey Closets, the world's first public toilets. For your penny you not only got a clean seat (a clean one, note!), but also a towel, a comb and a shoeshine. More than 800,000 people parted with their coppers over the next five-and-a-half months, and when the exhibition finished the closets remained open, raking in £1,000 per year.

BUT ... WHAT ABOUT ME?

 It might seem odd now, but many Dads are old enough to remember when the only live football match on television all year was the FA Cup final, broadcasting of which began in 1938. Luckily for us, one of the greatest cup finals was captured on film on this day in 1953, by which time an increasing number of the population had access to a TV (many acquired in anticipation of the Queen's Coronation later that summer). Football fans were treated to a seven-goal thriller as Blackpool beat Bolton Wanderers 4–3. Poor Stan Mortensen scored a hat-trick only to see the match dubbed 'The Matthews Final' in honour of his much-loved team-mate.

JUST FOR THE HELLESPONT OF IT

Most Dads are a bit mad, a few are bad, but not many are dangerous to know. Lord Byron was famously described as all three by Lady Caroline Lamb, but he was only a danger to himself today in 1810 when, emulating the mythical Leander, he swam the narrow but current swirling stretch of water separating Europe from Asia. It was then known as the Hellespont ('Sea of Hell') but is now called the Dardanelles. Whether he did it for a dare, a thrill, to show that it could be done or to prove his manliness despite his deformed foot, it was some feat.

BRITISH IS BETTER

On this day in 1893, cowboy Bill Pickett supposedly invented 'bulldogging', the rodeo technique of grabbing cattle by the horns and wrestling them to the ground. Goodness knows what made him think that was a sensible idea, but if that act somehow ultimately inspired the playground game of British Bulldog, then it was certainly a good day. The thought of a yard full of small boys charging past the 'bulldog' while he variously tries to tag, tackle, hold or lift them (depending on local rules) is enough to send Dads misty-eyed with nostalgia.

QUEEN OF THE AIR

In the 1930s pioneering aviatrix Amy Johnson had Britain spellbound with her aerial achievements. Luckily she had a Dad who supported her all the way in her flying ambitions; today in 1930 (despite only having gained her full pilot's licence in July 1929) she set off from Croydon in her Gypsy Moth plane. Nineteen days later she landed in Darwin to become the first female pilot to fly single-handed from England to Australia. After a decade of record-breaking flights, Amy died in a mysterious wartime crash in the Thames Estuary in 1941.

BOIL ME AN EGG, I'M GOING FOR A RUN

Athlete Roger Bannister didn't need an egg-timer – if he wanted a four-minute egg he just had to run a mile while it boiled. Perfect. Today in 1954 at Iffley Road, Oxford, he broke a running landmark that a number of other athletes had been closing in on for a couple of years – only one person would be able to claim the honour of being the first sub-four-minute miler. The record time was confirmed by timekeeper Norris McWhirter, who would go on to make his own name with the *Guinness Book of Records*, that compendium of largely useless feats so beloved of Dads.

SAY CHEESE (2)

Before today in 1888 Dads could only dream of lining the whole family up against the wall and shooting them – but from now they really could, thanks to George Eastman patenting his Kodak Box Camera. It had a fixed focal length and to change the film the device had to be returned to the factory, but it was still a great step forward for anyone wanting to take their own snaps. Eastman's motto was: 'You press the button, we do the rest.' Why Eastman called it Kodak, now a household name, is a mystery – it was dreamed up by him out of the blue.

THANKS, DAD

In 1896 Halsey Taylor's father died from typhoid fever, caused by contaminated water. Perhaps this was what inspired Taylor to dedicate himself to providing clean water to the American public, and on this day in 1912 he filed a patent for a drinking fountain and opened a factory in Ohio. He provided the innovative 'double bubbler' to the US Government for use by troops in World War One, and the Halsey Taylor company is still going strong today.

BLOOD AT THE TOWER

Dads love a good jewel-heist story, and one of the first and most audacious was today in 1671 by the infamous Colonel Thomas Blood. This shameless Anglo-Irish adventurer had switched sides in the Civil War, deserting King Charles I, so was forced to flee England when Charles II was restored. He returned in disguise and today, having earlier cased the joint dressed as a parson, he persuaded the keeper of the jewels to show him the collection. Despite Blood beating up the custodian, smashing and squashing the jewels to fit inside his trousers, and shooting at the guards who managed to apprehend him, he was pardoned by Charles II and granted a pension!

DON'T TRY THIS AT HOME, DAD!

Benjamin Franklin is famous for doing something so daft even a Dad wouldn't attempt it, namely flying a kite in a thunderstorm to prove his theories on electricity. Except he didn't. Franklin was a clever chap, far too clever to do anything that dense. What he probably did (his paperwork is a bit vague) was to fly a kite on a cloudy day to see if he could measure anything with the potential to make lightning. And today in 1752 a contemporary and friend of Franklin's, Thomas-François Dalibard, used a 12m (40ft) metal rod to extract electricity from a low cloud at Marly-la-Ville, France.

ROY'S RECORD-BREAKER

On this day in 1985, broadcasting legend Roy Plomley interviewed actress Sheila Steafel for Radio 4's *Desert Island Discs*. It was the 1,791st edition of the show Plomley had devised back in 1941, and it would be his last, as he died later that month aged 71. The UK's longest-running radio show is still going strong, and by the time you read this should have clocked up its 3,000th episode. What Dad can hear the strains of Eric Coates' 'By the Sleepy Lagoon' without wishing he was lying on a tropical beach with nothing for company but his eight favourite records, a good book and his little luxury?

NEARLY TIME FOR LUNCH ...

... which is when the Magna Carta was signed (15 June 1215, i.e. a quarter past twelve) by King John, having been issued with an ultimatum by his barons today in the same year. Showing all the courage and determination you might expect from his caricatures in various Robin Hood films down the years, John caved in and signed the famous document that limited his powers, strengthened the hand of the barons and, unsurprisingly, did not much for the little man. Still, its symbolism is still with us centuries later. And all Dads know *where* the Magna Carta was signed ... at the bottom.

SCHICK'S SLICK TRICK SAYS NIX TO NICKS

Ham-fisted Dads everywhere breathed a sigh of relief on this day in 1930 when Colonel Jacob Schick patented his dry electric razor, meaning those little dabs of tissues pasted on shaving cuts would soon be a thing of the past. The colonel first had the idea before World War One when he was recuperating from a gold-prospecting injury in Alaska, but his ideas for such a device were rejected by manufacturers – maybe it was the grapefruit-sized motor that put them off. But by 1930 he'd refined his idea enough to show that he was a cut above the competition.

JENNER BEATS THE POX

Dads hate it when their kids are ill, so the more that can be done to stop it the better. And one disease it's definitely good to see the back of is smallpox. A few people had noticed a connection between this killer and the less serious cowpox, but today in 1796, Edward Jenner was the first to do something about it when, unethically, he inoculated eight-year-old James Phipps with cowpox pus. A few weeks later he tried to pass on the smallpox virus to the boy but it wouldn't take. Vaccinations took a huge step forward, and in 1979 the world was declared smallpox-free.

STRICTLY SEQUINS

It's a funny old world, you know. Back in the 1970s and '80s the female dance troupes on *Top of the Pops* were considered pretty hot stuff, and when the raunchy Hot Gossip were thrust to fame via *The Kenny Everett Television Show* the complaints flooded in. But nowadays some of the costumes (barely) worn on the hit BBC show *Strictly Come Dancing*, which first aired today in 2004, are just as risqué, yet it passes for wholesome family entertainment – no wonder Brucie was so reluctant to step down. So Dads can sit on the sofa pretending to moan about the show, and still appreciate a well-executed fleckerl and a shapely ankle.

DO YOU THINK I'M MAD, DAD?

Today in 1990 was one of those events Dads can point to as evidence that, however daft they are, other Dads are worse (see also 19 November). At the height of the BSE/Mad Cow Disease controversy, Minister of Agriculture John Gummer thought it would be a terrific idea to show everyone how safe British beef was by force-feeding his daughter with a scalding-hot burger at a country show. Little Cordelia Gummer showed she had far more sense than her Dad by turning her nose up at it, and the photo-op turned into a PR disaster.

WHAT A CLUCKING WHOPPER

On this day in 2008 an ostrich on a farm in Sweden laid an egg weighing 2.589kg (5lb 11.36oz), setting the official Guinness World Record for the largest egg ever laid by a living bird. In 1896 a chicken in Lancashire apparently laid a 30cm (12in) long egg weighing nearly 340g (12oz); this would be chicken-feed to an ostrich but must have been eye-watering for the poor fowl. As your typical Dad would observe, what happened to the chicken that laid a record-breaking egg? It won the Pullet Surprise!

HOP IT!

In 1865, years before his celebrated creations Tom Sawyer and Huckleberry Finn appeared, Mark Twain had his first big success with the short story 'The Celebrated Jumping Frog of Calaveras County'. In 1950 an opera was staged based on the story. The actual frog-jumping contest in Angel's Camp, Calaveras County still takes place today. The funny thing is, the first contest wasn't held until this day in 1928, more than 60 years *after* the story was written. It's a tribute to all things Twain-related, with added frogs, and sounds like the sort of thing Dads would love.

ONE DOWN, IGNORAMUS (3 LETTERS)

What Dad wouldn't want to belong to the famous Baker Street Irregulars, Sherlock Holmes' trusty band of spies? Well, from 1934 you could. The only snag was that you had to solve a crossword puzzle in today's *Saturday Review of Literature* to be eligible for this new club, so you had to be a bit brainy. Most Dads get even the simplest crossword clues wrong: for example, 'Intercourse, four letters, ending in k', is obviously 'talk', not ... Still, as the club's activities seem to consist of discussing obscure Sherlockian questions rather than watching the latest Cumberbatch DVD, I don't suppose we're missing much.

DAD'S GOT THE BLUES

Dads have a pretty simple dress code: office? Suit. Anywhere else? Jeans. So it was a great day in 1873 when Jacob Davis teamed up with Levi Strauss to patent their copper-studded denim clothing. It took a while (until the 1950s, actually) before jeans caught on as leisurewear, but once they did there was no stopping them. The Levi Strauss company operates worldwide and is now just one of countless jeans manufacturers, but their famous 501s are still 'the Original'. Opinion is divided as to whether the best way of looking after jeans is to wash them, freeze them, bake them or just leave them to get filthy.

SUMMERTIME, AND THE LIVING IS ... EARLY

Dads love that extra hour they get in bed in the autumn, forgetting they paid for it when the clocks went forward in the spring. It all began today in 1916 as part of the war effort to save coal; if William Willett, the man who had long campaigned for the measure to make the most of daylight but who died in 1915, had had his way, the country would have put the clocks forward by 20 minutes every weekend for a month, which seems to be over-complicating it a bit.

NOW WHERE DID I PUT MY GLASSES?

Squeamish Dads, look away now – while those who quite like performing a bit of first aid on cuts and bruises could pick up a few tips. Today in 2014 at the Royal London Hospital, Shafi Ahmed performed the first operation streamed live online using Google Glasses. He removed cancerous tissue from the liver and bowel of 78-year-old Roy Pulfer while 13,000 medical students around the world watched; they could even type questions to the surgeon while he worked.

PICK A WINDOW, YOU'RE LEAVING!

We've already touched on Dads' sketchy historical knowledge and their penchant for snappy titles to keep them interested (see 28 January). Well, the Defenestration of Prague today in 1618 must be up there with the Diet of Worms. From the Latin word *fenestra* (window), defenestration means to throw someone out of a window, and that's exactly what happened to three Catholic bigwigs. In fact, this was the *second* DoP – the citizens of Prague had a practice in 1419, and obviously developed a taste for it. Although the 1618 victims survived a 21-m (70ft) drop (either by a miracle or a handily placed dung-heap, take your pick), the incident led to the Thirty Years' War.

I BET HE'S BIN CELEBRATING

On this day in 2014 39-year-old wheelie-bin cleaner Craig Brazier won £1.3m for a £2 stake on horse-racing's Scoop6, one of the biggest betting-shop wins in history. You could tell he was a Dad: he likes a flutter and he likes fishing (he placed the bet with a couple of quid he had left after buying maggots). But he obviously didn't win quite enough to retire, as he said he definitely wasn't giving up the day job. And although he missed out on a bonus £5m the following week, he was content, saying, 'I can chill out now and enjoy the rest of my life.' Dad heaven.

I'LL DO IT, JUST GIVE ME EIGHT YEARS

Can you imagine the response if your Dad announced in advance his intention to re-grout the bathroom 'within five years'? So it seems unfair that when President John F. Kennedy, today in 1961, set himself a timetable of 'by the end of the decade', he was met with acclaim and plaudits. Granted, he had just announced to Congress the intention of the US to land a man on the Moon and return him safely, but I think it's the principle that counts. Against all the odds, NASA met JFK's target with five months to spare (see 20 July), and the Space Age had well and truly begun.

NOW, WHAT CAN I DO WITH IT ...?

Dads dream of inventing something life-changing, simple but useful, like self-finding keys or a time machine. Then they could patent it and become rich! But you wonder quite what scientists Klaus Fuchs and John von Neumann thought they could gain when they filed a secret patent today in 1946 for their hydrogen bomb. Were they hoping the Soviets would pay them royalties to use it? As it turned out, Fuchs had already decided to cut out the middle-man and was passing weapons information to Russia. He confessed in 1950 and was imprisoned; on his release in 1959 he immigrated to East Germany.

CLINT CATCHES ON

Baltimore baseball catcher Clint Courtney ticks just about every Dad box you could imagine. Hygienically, he was a cattle farmer who rarely washed, commenting to a room-mate surprised at his suitcase full of already dirty clothes, 'We'll only be gone six days'. Easy to trick and wind up, but useless in a fight, he was myopic and his cavorting on the field was likened to 'a waiter serving pizza on roller skates'. He was so daft he would stop the ball with his head if necessary. And today in 1960 he decided to even the odds a bit by using a catching mitt 50 per cent bigger than anyone else's!

RUST TURNS RED

How many Dads dream of hopping into the car and just seeing where they end up? That's more or less what German teenager Mathias Rust did on this day in 1987 when he got in his Cessna aeroplane in Helsinki, told air-traffic control he was going to Stockholm, then headed for Moscow. It was his lucky day – the Soviet jets scrambled to tail him didn't shoot him down; the trolley wires strung on the bridge where he landed near Red Square had been taken down for maintenance that morning; and the prevailing spirit of *glasnost* and *perestroika* meant he didn't spend the next 20 years in a gulag, though it was 14 months before he was released back to the West.

HAPPY CHRISTMAS!

Yes, I know it's a bit early, but in 1660 Dads hadn't been able to celebrate their favourite holiday for 16 years, since Oliver Cromwell and his fellow Puritans had taken umbrage at the drunkenness and revelry that often accompanied Christmas celebrations, as well as what they considered its Papist links. Today, on his 30th birthday, King Charles II was welcomed back to London after the fall of the English Commonwealth – the monarchy was restored and with it the Twelve Days of Christmas.

GIVE 'EM WAT FOR

Today in 1381 John Bampton arrived in Brentwood, Essex, to gather unpaid poll taxes. It all got a bit out of hand, Bampton was chased back to London, and all of a sudden the 'Peasants' Revolt' against excessive taxation was under way. Wat Tyler was elected leader and the rebels marched on the capital, executing the hated Lord Chancellor, Simon Sudbury. King Richard II was forced to promise concessions, but in a fittingly messy dénouement Tyler was killed and the rebellion quashed. On the plus side, it led to the following awful Dad joke: Who led the Pedants' Revolt? *Which* Tyler.

DADS ARE COOL – IT'S OFFICIAL

On this day in 1976, at the height of the disco boom, Boney M (from Jamaica, via Germany … try and keep up) found fame in the UK when they released the song that would become their debut hit, 'Daddy Cool'. They went on to have a successful career, including two number ones ('Rivers of Babylon' and 'Mary's Boy Child'), but none had the same impact on Dads as that first one. It's described somewhat cruelly on Wikipedia as a 'novelty gimmick record', but we Dads know the hidden truth it speaks.

JUNE

WATER OF LIFE

How appropriate: *aqua vitae* in Latin, *uisge beatha* in the Gaelic, long since shortened to 'whisky'. The first reference to it is from Ireland, when a chieftain's death in 1405 was ascribed to 'a surfeit of aqua vitae'. In Scotland it was first mentioned today in 1454 in the Rolls of the Royal Exchequer, when a certain friar was sent a quantity of malt to turn into the golden liquid. There are now 109 distilleries in Scotland licensed to produce whisky. Dads like to think they're connoisseurs, but most couldn't tell the difference between Johnnie Walker Black Label and supermarket own-label.

THE BATTLE OF SANTIAGO

Dads love seeing a good sporting punch-up. They'll watch boxing at a pinch, but they much prefer it when mayhem breaks out in other sports. On this day in the 1962 FIFA World Cup hosts Chile played Italy in a nasty encounter refereed by Englishman Ken Aston. The first player was sent off after just 12 minutes, and the match was full of spitting, snarling and punching. Unfortunately, Aston missed most of the Chilean provocation and concentrated on sending off Italians for retaliation. He blamed his linesman, saying he'd refused to tell him what he'd seen! Between the assault and battery a football match broke out occasionally, with Chile winning 2–0.

IT'S NEVER TOO LATE (1)

In 1899 the great W.G. Grace made his final appearance for England in a Test match against Australia at Trent Bridge, only a month short of his 51st birthday. He's still the third-oldest Test cricketer on record and, amazingly, a young chap making his debut in that match went on to become the oldest one ever Wilfred Rhodes (52½ in his last match in 1930). And the oldest Test match debutant was 49-year-old James Southerton in 1877 – so for any Dads under 50, there's still hope!

IT SEEMED LIKE SUCH A GOOD IDEA

When the Cleveland Indians baseball team decided to boost crowds by offering a 'Ten Cent Beer Night', what could possibly go wrong? How many of the 25,000 crowd – twice the usual number – that turned up today in 1974 were baseball fans and how many were stray Dads tempted by cheap beer is hard to say. But the drunken antics that followed resulted in streaking, missile-throwing and finally a mass riot on the pitch; it was a disaster for Cleveland, who ended up forfeiting the match and facing a massive repair bill.

GREAT INVENTION …
NOW HOW DO WE GET IT OFF?

Hail to William Painter, inventor and inductee into the US Inventor Hall of Fame in 2006 – and surely he must have been a Dad. Among his 85 patented inventions was one filed in 1889 for a device to put crown tops on beer bottles to keep the contents lovely and fresh … just what every Dad needs. The only trouble was, like many Dads, it seems William had rather put the cart before the horse, because it wasn't until this day in 1893 that he filed a patent for a bottle *opener*. How many frustrated thirsty drinkers were awaiting his second invention is not recorded.

ALL TOGETHER NOW

Today in 1844 George Williams, a London draper, founded an organisation intended to improve the 'spiritual condition of young men' who were being distracted by the inns and brothels of the city. As well as the less-enticing prayer and bible-reading groups, the fledgling Young Men's Christian Association offered sports and athletics clubs – so-called 'muscular Christianity'. Within a few years the YMCA had spread throughout Europe and North America. You could say it was an instant hit, just like the Village People's tune that got to number one in 1979 and still gets Dads practising their 'semaphore dance' to this day.

ALL THE WORLD'S A STAGE

Inside every Dad there's a ham actor trying to get out, and what better place to tread the boards than the faithful reproduction of Shakespeare's famous Globe Theatre. It was the dream of US Anglophile film director Sam Wanamaker, who died in 1993 before he could see his dream realised. It is located on the south bank of the River Thames, just a short distance from the site of the original building. Conceived by Wanamaker in 1969, on this day in 1997 it officially opened its doors to drama lovers, who stand in the open air for performances (unless they shell out extra for seats in the balconies).

'I THINK WE JUST PASSED IT'

Dads' sense of direction can sometimes be a few miles out (see 23 March), but what happened today in 1965 proves they could be worse. The Russians were arguably ahead of the USA in the Space Race at this point – today they launched Luna 6, which would try to land a robot module on the Moon. From the Baikonur Cosmodrome in the deserts of Kazakhstan they took aim and fired Luna 6 at that big shiny thing in the sky about 3,200km (2,000 miles) across … and missed. By about 160,000km (99,000 miles). It flew right past the Moon and, as far as anyone knows, it's still out there somewhere.

WHAT DID YOU SAY YOUR NAME WAS?

There is constant debate in many families about whether communication problems are caused by mumbling kids or deaf Dads – and a house with several kids is as noisy as it gets. Thankfully, for anyone hard of hearing we have Action on Hearing Loss (2011), formerly known as the Royal National Institution for Deaf People (1992), formerly the Royal National Institute for the Deaf (1961), formerly the National Institute for the Deaf (1924), which began life today in 1911 as the National Bureau for Promoting the General Welfare of the Deaf. Try and keep up …

ARE YOU SURE THEY WERE BLANKS?

Whether it's Bonfire Night, New Year's Eve or whatever, Dads love making a big bang, don't they? Today in 1975 some bright spark at the New York Yankees decided it would be a great idea to commemorate the US Army's 200th birthday with a 21-gun salute before their game against the California Angels at the Shea Stadium. The cannons made a hell of a noise, as intended, and when the smoke cleared it became apparent that the blast wave from the guns had been enough to topple the outfield fence. Oops.

MARXISM RULES!

If you want to keep a Dad of a certain type out of your way for a couple of hours, just sit him down in front of a Marx Brothers movie. Their quick-fire gags combined with stupid slapstick made them huge stars in the 1930s. Today in 1937 MGM released their seventh film, *A Day at The Races*, which included the famous Groucho line 'Either he's dead or my watch has stopped.' He played the wacky Dr Hackenbush – it was originally 'Quackenbush', but then they discovered there really was a Dr Quackenbush. (You might find it hard to credit, but Google it and you'll find there are still Quackenbushes in the US!)

DON'T BASH DADS – THAT'S OUR JOB!

On this day in 2013 Dads who feel they get a raw deal in the media were given a boost from an unlikely source – Netmums. A poll of 2,000 Mums stuck up for their partners by agreeing that cartoons and other TV shows portray fathers in a bad light, with 93 per cent agreeing that children's shows such as *The Simpsons* and *The Flintstones* don't represent real-life Dads (you don't say ...). Netmums founder Siobhan Freegard said, 'The type of jokes aimed at Dads would be banned if they were aimed at women ... there's nothing amusing about taking away good role models for young boys.'

FIRST-CLASS MALE ... OR FEMALE

From today in 1920, American Dads looking to save a few bob were saved from themselves. Up until then, some parsimonious Pas had realised that it was cheaper to send small children by post than to cough up for a rail fare, and the temptation was too much for some of them. The nippers would travel with stamps attached to their clothes rather than buying a rail ticket. As from this day, the option was closed off as it finally became illegal in the US to send children through the mail.

I DO LIKE TO BE BESIDE THE SEASIDE

With airline queues, missing luggage and screaming kids, you can't beat a holiday in Britain nowadays. And what better way to do it than with a caravan? Whether holed up in a static van with rain beating a comforting staccato on the roof, or crawling along the A303 towing a tin-can on wheels at the head of an endless tailback, there's fun to be had for all the family. But Dads who think the 'caravan rally' they're off to will give them a chance to race other owners round a muddy field will be disappointed – they're just the regular get-togethers of the Caravan Club, formed on this day in 1907.

YES? NO? MAYBE?

In the 2010 FIFA World Cup, English Dads watched aghast as a clear Frank Lampard 'goal' against Germany wasn't given by the officials. Move forward four years to Brazil, and on this day FIFA's new toy, goal-line technology, had its first big test when a France shot against the post rolled along the line only for the Honduran goalkeeper to knock it just over. GLT correctly called 'no-goal' for the shot and 'goal' for the deflection, but it was too complicated for BBC commentator Jonathan Pearce (the only person in the world who didn't understand what had happened), whose bafflement had viewers in stitches.

SCARY MOVIE

It's film time again, and an enduring tale of the trials and tribulations of a Dad whose daughter is about to be married. *Father of the Bride* began life as a 1949 novel, was made into a successful film (released today in 1950) starring Spencer Tracy, and a quick follow-up, *Father's Little Dividend*, was also made. It was remade in 1991 with Steve Martin in the title role, with a sequel following in 1995. In 2014 it was reported that a third film in the series is being planned, this time, topically, with gay marriage at its heart.

DODGING THE LAW
AND HOOVERING UP PROFITS

There are few names more resonant of the Wild West than Dodge City, christened after nearby Fort Dodge, run by a US colonel of the same name. He banned the sale of alcohol at the fort, affecting not only the soldiers but the traders and hunters in the area and the workers on the new railroad. On this day in 1872, an enterprising fellow called George M. Hoover spotted an opportunity, bought a wagonload of whiskey and set up shop 8km (five miles) away from the fort. The town sprang up and the legends soon attached themselves to it – Boot Hill, Wyatt Earp, Doc Holliday etc. – keeping Western-loving Dads entertained for years.

WATERLOO SUNSET

Napoleon met his Waterloo and disappeared into the sunset today in 1815, when the forces of the Duke of Wellington and Field Marshal Blücher defeated him on a battlefield in present-day Belgium. Wellington withstood the French Army throughout the day until the arrival of Blücher's troops swung the battle the Allies' way. It was 'the nearest-run thing you ever saw in your life', according to the Iron Duke. And it was great for Dads, firstly because 1815 is one of the few dates they can remember, and secondly for the old joke: Where did Napoleon keep his armies? Up his sleevies!

'ELLO, 'ELLO, 'ELLO

Dads are sometimes a bit suspicious of the police, mainly because whenever they see an authority figure (like Mum, for instance) they automatically feel guilty, even in the unlikely event they've done nothing wrong. But it's always good to know you can call on them when you need it, so today in 1829 it was good news when the Robert Peel's Metropolitan Police Act was passed, the founding of policing as we know it in the UK. The principles of unarmed officers distinctive from the military was laid down from the start, and now we all feel a bit safer when we see a bobby on the beat.

WHO'S WHO, LOU?

Older Dads will remember wet summer holidays spent watching endless showings of black-and-white comedy films on the BBC. And some of the most popular were American funnymen Bud Abbott and Lou Costello. In a long series of movies they bumped into all sorts of characters: Captain Kidd, Frankenstein, the Mummy, Jekyll and Hyde etc. Admittedly their brand of comedy hasn't aged too well, but their classic 'Who's On First?' sketch is still a perfect example of comedy timing. It featured in the film *The Naughty Nineties*, released today in 1945.

TAKE MY DAUGHTER ... PLEASE!

A cautionary tale for Dads tempted to selfless acts of bravery – you might get more than you bargained for. Today in 1854 Charles Lucas was a humble midshipman aboard the *Hecla* during the Crimean War with Russia. The *Hecla* was attacking the fort of Bomarsund when a live enemy shell landed on deck. Ignoring shouts to take cover, Lucas picked up the shell and threw it overboard. For this he was promoted to Lieutenant (he ended up a Rear-Admiral) and received the very first Victoria Cross. Twenty-five years later he married the daughter of the *Hecla*'s captain that day, William Hall, after Hall had asked Lucas to do so on his deathbed!

AND YET IT MOVES ...

We've all been there, Dads. You know you're right – it's just easier to say that you're wrong rather than stay in the doghouse. Today in 1633 Galileo had a similar problem, except there was a bit more at 'stake', as he might well have been burned to a crisp for heresy had he not recanted his ridiculous support for the Copernican theory that the Earth moved round the Sun whereas any fool – the Inquisition, for instance – knew that the opposite was the case. By publicly retracting his opinions, Galileo was able to at least live a quiet life under house arrest.

GOODBYE, HARRIET

She was old, bald and slow, so would have made a great companion for a Dad – except she would have seen off several generations of Dads, because Harriet the Galapagos tortoise died in Australia Zoo, Queensland, on this day in 2006 aged about 176. Captured by Charles Darwin in 1835, poor Harriet was thought to be male for a while – until 1960 in fact. Prior to that, she had been introduced to several other female tortoises in failed mating attempts, before a zookeeper from Honolulu arrived and duly pointed out their mistake.

IS IT BETAMAX OR VHS?

Younger readers might not remember a time before DVDs and iPlayers, but there was a time in the distant past when if you wanted to record your favourite TV programme you used a (frequently chewed-up) video cassette. They started to catch on in the mid-1970s, and the format war that followed was a nasty business, with VHS finally wiping out its rival, Betamax. But it all started today in 1963, when the Nottingham produced Telcan home recording system was demonstrated at the BBC's Alexandra Palace. It cost £60 (over £1,000 in current value), but for that you could tape a whopping 20 minutes of telly.

OH, HANOVER!

There was much to admire about Prince Albert, who became Prince Consort to Queen Victoria today in 1857: he was a handsome, attentive, potent husband (they had nine children), a loving Dad, and seemed to care greatly for his adopted nation. What a pity about his surname that he passed on to his son King Edward VII: Saxe-Coburg and Gotha (not Hall, as many Dads think). It was hard to spell, a bit of a mouthful and (when World War One came along) a bit too German for most people's liking, which is why in 1917 it was changed to the much more English-sounding Windsor.

HE WHO FAILS TO PAY THE PIPER ...

Dads might like the idea of a house without any kids – for a day or two the peace would be delightful. But the citizens of Hamelin got more peace than they bargained for today in 1284 when, according to legend, the Pied Piper enchanted away 130 children after not being paid for a rat-catching job. A complete myth? Maybe, but there is a mysterious first reference to something funny happening in the town chronicles in 1384 that says baldly (and unhelpfully): 'It is 100 years since our children left ...' Whether the children were lost to disease, disaster or devilish pipers, no one knows.

DO YOU TAKE A CHEQUE?

No one likes spending money, Dads least of all, but there are times when we all need a bit of cash – so it's hard to remember that it wasn't so long ago that if you wanted some of the folding stuff for a night in the pub, you had to take a cheque to your bank (only open 9.30–3.30, and not on Saturdays) and queue up behind all the other poor souls using their lunch hour to get some readies. So what a relief on this day in 1967 when comedy actor Reg Varney made the world's first cash withdrawal from a hole in the wall outside Barclays Bank in Enfield. On the downside, it did remove one of Dad's favourite excuses for not doling out pocket money: 'The bank's shut'.

NOW YOU SEE IT ...

Many Dads are unsettled by coincidences – for instance, they can't accept that the moon and the sun appearing the same size in the sky isn't 'significant' in some way. But it was for the Native Americans today in 1451, when a total solar eclipse might have played a part in preventing war between the traditional 'Five Nations' tribes: the Senecas, Cayugas, Onondagas, Oneidas and Mohawks. This was around the time of Hiawatha and legend has it that he and Deganawida (the Great Peacemaker) interpreted the eclipse as a sign that the tribes should unite, not fight.

TOP OF THE POPS

29 The most popular musical recording on this day in 1888 was Georg Friedrich Handel's oratorio *Israel in Egypt*. If that seems an unlikely hit, I should point out that as far as we know it was the very first musical recording of any kind, preserved for posterity on a paraffin cylinder at the Crystal Palace Handel Festival by Colonel George Gourand, Thomas Edison's European sales agent. Whether Victorian Dads were shouting upstairs to their teenage children to 'Turn that blasted Handel down' is not recorded …

I COULD DO THAT BLINDFOLDED

30 Such is the typical response of any Dad to a feat that fails to impress them. But after crossing Niagara Falls on a 305m (1,000ft) long tightrope for the first time today in 1859, Jean-François Gravelet, more famously known as 'The Great Blondin', repeated the stunt with variations several times in later crossings: with his manager on his back; on stilts; pushing a wheelbarrow; dressed as a gorilla; and, of course, blindfolded. He survived these and many other feats of funambulism and died in London in 1897 at the age of 72.

JULY

FAGS VERY MUCH

A great day for Dads today in 2007 as they could finally take their kids into a pub or restaurant for a meal without having to worry about passive smoking – or them all coming out with their clothes smelling of stale cigarette smoke. The ban on smoking in public places came into force in England, and five years on the benefits were already beginning to be felt – a study of bar workers found their respiratory health had 'greatly improved', and in an opinion poll 78 per cent of the public supported the restrictions.

IS THE TRUTH OUT THERE?

Dads love a good alien conspiracy theory, and the mother of them all was Roswell 1947. It's so shrouded in mystery that people can't even agree on what happened and when: was it June or July (it might have been today)? Was there one crash or two? Was it a little green man, a top-secret weapon or a new type of weather balloon? The official story since the 1990s has been that it was a failure of a hush-hush project to monitor Soviet nuclear tests. Or maybe that's just what they want Dads to believe …

BACK TO THE … DRAWING BOARD

Dads love a flash car, preferably one too small to fit any kids in, and the flashiest of them all was perhaps the DeLorean DMC-12 (not sure why they bothered with the DMC-12 – it was the only car the company ever built) with its super-cool, space-age gull-wing doors. It was built just outside the thrusting go-ahead city of Belfast, thanks to those canny chaps at the Northern Ireland Development Agency throwing £100 million at them. Production began in January 1981 and, sure enough, bankruptcy followed in late 1982. A pity they couldn't have kept going until this day in 1985, when *Back to the Future* gave the DeLorean the sort of publicity you couldn't buy.

GROUNDHOG DAY

Given the choice, the last day of the week Dads would want *two* of would be Mondays. When some bright spark decided it would be good for the Samoan Islands to jump to the other side of the International Date Line in 1892 (to align with the US) it meant they would have to repeat a day somewhere. Surprisingly, instead of taking the opportunity for a three-day weekend they opted for a double dose of Monday 4 July. In 2011, Samoa (by now separate from American Samoa) jumped back again and 'lost' Friday 30 December – in other words, a day of the Christmas holidays! Great planning, guys.

THE FIRST FATHER'S DAY

In December 1907, the Monongah Mining Disaster in West Virginia killed 361 men, 250 of whom were fathers; on this day the following year the Williams Memorial Methodist Episcopal Church South observed the first Father's Day in their memory. Over the following decades several attempts were made (supported keenly by the greetings cards and gift industries, for some reason) to establish the event on the official calendar of the USA, but it wasn't until 1972 that President Richard Nixon made it a national holiday, and now Dads everywhere are guaranteed their burned toast and cold tea in bed on the third Sunday in June.

THE BALLOON NOW BOARDING ...

If you had the choice between hurtling down a strip of Tarmac at 320kph (200mph) in a metal tube, praying that you'd take off before you ran out of runway, or gently lifting off and floating down again, which would you pick? Even for Dads, it's a no-brainer. So what an achievement today in 1919 when the first crossing of the Atlantic by airship was achieved by the British R34 when it arrived in Long Island. Strangely, because no one on the ground knew how to handle an airship landing, a crew member had to parachute down to show them!

THE BEST THING SINCE ... ERM ...

Contrary to popular belief, Dads aren't lazy, just always seeking ways to save time to devote to useful stuff like ... Well, anyway, 7 July 1928 was a great day for everyone when the first machine-sliced and machine-wrapped loaves of bread went on sale in the USA. Otto Rohwedder's invention was first used by the Chillicothe Baking Company in Missouri and in just five years US production of sliced bread had overtaken its old-fashioned, un-sliced alternative.

LET'S DANCE

On this day in 1957, the *Manchester Guardian* proved it had its finger on the pulse of modern youth by reporting: 'The scooter-riding, blue-jeans, coca-cola-drinking, disco-club young things are hotly modern in tendency.' According to the OED, this is perhaps the first recorded use of the word 'disco' in print. It certainly reads like the *Guardian* – see that typo where the reporter meant to write 'blue-jeans-*wearing*'? Those 'young things' naturally grew up to be Dads, and they've hardly stopped dancing since (though they ceased to be 'hotly modern' in 1958), pausing only to pass on their skills to the Dads of the future.

READY, STEADY, MOW!

In a Sussex pub in 1973, Irishman Jim Gavin's thoughts turned to motor racing, and how he could get involved on a limited budget. His gaze travelled from the Cricketers Arms to the cricket pitch outside, and the groundsman mowing the wicket. In a flash of inspiration the British Lawn Mower Racing Association was born, and has since gone from strength to strength. On this day in 2014 Julie Walters dropped the flag to start the highlight of its calendar, the 12-hour Endurance Race, won by the 'Northerners Kick Grass' team. Can there be a Dad reading this whose throttle fingers aren't twitching at the thought of taking part?

SEASIDE SAUCINESS

Donald McGill was a perfectly respectable naval draughtsman until 1904, when his sideline of hand-drawn cards took off. He's now renowned as the 'king of the saucy postcard', the sort Dads love to send back from the seaside. His postcard of a bookish chap asking a girl, 'Do you like Kipling?' and getting the reply, 'I don't know … I've never kippled,' sold six million copies, a world record. Despite this, he was paid in flat fees, not royalties, and died a poor man in 1962. Today in 2010 his grandson Patrick Tumber opened the Donald McGill Postcard Museum in Ryde on the Isle of Wight.

CLUELESS (1)

With a title that could have been designed for them, and more awful puns than you could shake some shtick at, *I'm Sorry, I Haven't A Clue* is the perfect Dads' radio show. Billed as 'the antidote to panel games' and beginning today in 1972, the show is still going strong despite having to cope with the loss of its original host, the peerless and multitalented Humphrey Lyttelton, in 2008. With rounds such as Sound Charades, the Uxbridge English Dictionary and the baffling Mornington Crescent, and its glamorous scorers Samantha and Sven, let's hope it supplies us with double entendres for years to come.

TORNADO? I'M NOT ALLOWED TO TELL YOU

That, unbelievably, was the strange state of affairs in the US until 1950. As far back as the 1880s, the government had banned the use of the word 'tornado' in weather forecasts for fear of causing panic among the population. In fairness, back then weather prediction was still in its infancy, and inaccurate warnings might well have caused more trouble than they prevented. However, the ban was still in place by 1950, when sanity finally prevailed today and the Weather Bureau lifted the restriction. Dads could now be told when they needed to dive into the cellar with their precious possessions (and, hopefully, their families).

THE FIRST NOWELL LOSES HIS BOTTLE

Dr Alexander Nowell was an extraordinary chap. He lived into his nineties, was an MP, the Dean of St Paul's and canon at Windsor Castle, and he annoyed Elizabeth I by preaching to her that she should marry. But what matters to us is that today in 1568 he made a serendipitous discovery. A few days earlier he had gone fishing and taken with him a bottle into which he'd poured some beer. Being a bit absent-minded, he mislaid his drink. Today he found it again and 'found it was still perfectly drinkable' – the forgetful friar had just discovered bottled beer!

IT'S A BIT COLDER THAN I EXPECTED ...

In 1789, as the French Revolution took off, far away in North America explorer Alexander Mackenzie was seeking to become the first person north of Mexico to reach the Pacific Coast from the east. He thought he'd found a likely-looking river and, following his nose in true Dad fashion, paddled his canoe all the way to the sea. He reached it today, but instead of the mighty Pacific he was disappointed to find it was only the Arctic Ocean. Refusing to be downhearted, four years later he eventually found the right river and the right ocean.

TOO SEXY FOR THIS BOOK

Think of Dad anthems and there are one or two that come to mind: 'You Ain't Seen Nothing Yet', 'I Will Survive', etc. But one that he will undoubtedly identify with (even though his voice is nowhere near low enough) is Right Said Fred's 'I'm Too Sexy', released this day in 1991. Lead singer Richard Fairbrass assured fans on his way to the top of the charts that he was too sexy for his love, his shirt, a party, his car, his hat, his cat and, finally, 'this song'. The band took their oblique name from the song that was a hit for Bernard Cribbins in 1965 (see 29 December).

I'D LOVE TO KISS YOU DEAR, BUT ...

In the 14th century the Black Death swept Europe, wiping out 30 to 60 per cent of the population. It had 'plagued' the continent on and off for centuries, and when it returned to England in 1439, King Henry VI was taking no chances. Although we realise now it was mainly transmitted by rats and fleas, Henry didn't know that and decided that osculatory exercises were too risky – so he banned kissing until the end of the 'plague season', as summers were known. Apart from the obvious thought that you wouldn't particularly want to kiss someone covered in buboes, there's no evidence that many people took much notice of the ban.

MADRAS TO CHENNAI, VIA LIMERICK

'There was a young maid of Madras, who had a magnificent ass; not rounded and pink as you'd probably think, it was grey, had long ears and ate grass!' This day in 1996 was not a good one for limerick-loving Dads, when the good people of Madras decided they wanted their city to be called Chennai from now on. Still, we'd had nearly 357 years to perfect that wonderful little ditty, since the little fishing village of Madraspatnam was taken over by the British East India Company. Now, I wonder if that old man from Chennai's got a glass eye …

GOD BLESS ST ARNULF

St Arnulf (or Arnold) of Metz, whose feast day is today, was a privileged military commander before becoming a bishop. But that's not why St Arnulf is favoured by Dads. In 642, the parishioners of Metz went to collect the remains of Arnulf from Remiremont Abbey, where he had died in 640. It was very hot, they had nothing to drink, and one of them remarked, 'By his powerful intercession the Blessed Arnold will bring us what we lack.' Lo and behold, an empty beer mug began to froth with ale, and there was plenty to see the thirsty pilgrims to their destination. Thus is Arnulf now the patron saint of brewers.

CLUELESS (2)

All Dads suffer from 'foot in mouth' syndrome from time to time, but did you know there is an annual award for it, presented by the Plain English Campaign? First awarded in 1993, George W. Bush received a 'lifetime achievement award' in 2008, and Boris Johnson won in 2004 when he uttered, 'I could not fail to disagree with you less.' But my favourite is Alicia Silverstone, star of the frothy comedy *Clueless* (released today in 1995), whose verdict on the film was: 'I think that *Clueless* was very deep. I think it was deep in the way that it was very light.' Spoken like a true Dad ...

ONE SMALL STEP FOR A DAD ...

Seeing as it's over 40 years in the past, a lot of you reading this probably weren't even born when Neil Armstrong became the first Dad to land on the moon on this day in 1969. He walked into history when he stepped out of the lunar module and planted his feet on the surface of another world, fluffing his lines when he uttered those famous 'One small step for [a] man' words. In true Dad style, having broken a vital switch when they re-entered the lunar module, Armstrong and Buzz Aldrin codged it up with a felt-tip pen. Just as well they didn't have to stop to ask for directions ...

FINALLY, SOMETHING THEY'RE GOOD FOR!

Dads have keenly tuned musical ears, and most kids who brought a set of bagpipes into the home would be quickly shown the door, but a good-news story from Scotland was reported in 2005 by the *Daily Record*. Thirteen-year-old asthma sufferer Richard Humphries found a big improvement in his condition when he took up the instrument. A spokesman for Asthma UK told the paper: 'Anything that makes someone with asthma take big, deep breaths to fill their lungs to capacity and teaches them to breathe out slowly helps.' Maybe they should be made available (with earplugs) on the NHS.

HENNY MAPPY RETURNS!

Yes, bappy hirthday (I'll stop now) to the man who gave his name to one of Dads' favourite word-mangling methods. Dr William Spooner was born today in 1844 and was a sometimes bewildered Oxford don, though most spoonerisms attributed to him are probably apocryphal. He once invited a fellow to tea '… to welcome Casson'. 'But I am Casson,' he replied. 'Never mind,' said Spooner, 'come anyway.' The most famous utterance he allegedly made was to a recalcitrant student: 'You have hissed all my mystery lectures, and were caught fighting a liar in the quad. Having tasted two worms, you will leave by the next town drain.'

AS EASY AS ABCFKNRST

Everyone's heard of the Ford Model T, launched in 1908 – it was probably your Dad's first car! Today in Chicago in 1903 Ernst Pfennig became the proud owner of Henry Ford's first production car, the Model A. So Henry must have got through another 18 models in five years, right? Wrong. The Model A was followed by Models B and C, but Henry, who famously said history was bunk, showed he hadn't done much work on the alphabet either, skipping to F, then K ... you get the picture. The follow-up to the Model T was, naturally, a new Model A.

SCHUBERT'S UNOPENED PARACHUTE

BASE jumping consists of parachuting from Buildings, Antennae, Spans (bridges) or Earth. Even Dads think it's bonkers. The first recognised BASE jump took place today in 1966 when Michael Pelkey and Brian Schubert jumped from the 900-m (2,950ft) El Capitan cliff in the Yosemite National Park. Their girlfriends were meant to photograph the event but sensibly got fed up of waiting and left. Schubert broke his legs on landing, which probably put him off, because his next BASE jump was 40 years later at a 'Bridge Day' event at New River Gorge, West Virginia. Sadly, this time his parachute failed to deploy properly and he was killed.

JUST WHAT I ALWAYS WANTED ...

On this day in 1893 a monument was unveiled in Dubrovnik to a hero of Croatian arts, the poet Ivan Gundulic (1589–1638). His epic poem *Osman* is considered a landmark in Croatian history (what do you mean you haven't read it?). He is of more interest to Dads, however, for his sartorial impact, because he was the first person known to have appeared in a portrait wearing a cravat; and the cravat (the very name comes from a French corruption of their name for 'Croat') was the forerunner of the necktie, that ubiquitous Christmas-present stand-by for desperate children everywhere. Thanks, Ivan ... thanks, kids.

DON'T GIVE DAD ANY IDEAS ...

Another nomination for World's Worst Dad here, courtesy of Johnny Cash. When he released his version of Shel Silverstein's 'A Boy Named Sue' on this day in 1969 it became one of his most popular records. The song (for younger readers) tells the story of a chap whose father named him Sue before running out on the family; Sue swears to track him down and kill him. When he finally meets his Dad they fight to a standstill before Pa reveals he named his son Sue to keep him tough. In a sentimental ending, Sue reflects, 'If I ever have a son, I think I'm gonna name him ... Bill or George, anything but Sue!'

NICE BUM!

In July 1970 any lusty Dad who wanted to see a bit of naked flesh had a tough job. The *Sun*'s Page Three was still months away. From today, though, he could nip down to the West End for a bit of 'culture' and see Kenneth Tynan's sex-based, nudity-filled revue *Oh! Calcutta!* It ran until 1980 and chalked up 3,918 performances. Writing contributions came from Samuel Beckett and John Lennon, among others, but it was always the prospect of thesps in the buff that was the attraction. The title came from a nude painting by Clovis Trouille, which was a pun on the French *'oh quel cul t'as!'* – 'what a lovely bum!'

YOUR CHEQUE'S IN THE ROCKET

You can keep your email and your Amazon drone deliveries. If an innovation tested today in the 1930s had come to fruition, Dads would be sending all their post in the coolest way possible – by rocket! The idea had been pushed around in the 19th century, but nothing had come of it. But by the late 1920s it seemed it was an idea whose time had come. After a few continental experiments, Gerhard Zucker launched two mail rockets between the Hebridean islands of Harris and Scarp, the first on this day in 1934 and the second three days later. The rockets both exploded, scattering the letters high and wide. Can't think why it didn't catch on ...

CHUNNEL VISION

Dads who are used to whizzing under the English Channel on Eurostar with the family on the way to the Continent nowadays should be grateful. Until the Tunnel was opened in 1994, queasy travellers who wanted to take their car abroad had to put up with the choppy waters of the Channel. The Treaty of Canterbury that made the scheme possible was ratified by PM Margaret Thatcher and President François Mitterrand today in 1987. No longer would there be the chance to trot out the apocryphal British newspaper headline: 'FOG IN CHANNEL: CONTINENT CUT OFF'.

ESCAPE TO VICTORY

Combine a war film with football and you've got a movie that will appeal to Dads everywhere. Never mind that the actors couldn't play football, the footballers couldn't act, the plot was daft and the ending was implausible. It's a war film ... about football ... with real footballers (including three World Cup winners – Bobby Moore, Pelé and Ossie Ardiles)! It was released on this day in 1981 and it was brilliant.

HOWZAT!

Perfection in sport, as in life, is something that rarely comes round – ask any Dad – but England spin bowler Jim Laker nearly managed it on this day in 1956. When he took the final wicket of the Ashes Test at Old Trafford he had taken 19 of the 20 Australian wickets to fall in the match, a world record for first-class cricket that has never been beaten. The 'villain' of the piece was Laker's England colleague Tony Lock, who dismissed Jim Burke in the first innings – the only wicket Laker failed to take. His Austrian wife was apparently underwhelmed; when he got in that night she said, 'Jim, did you do something good today?'

AUGUST

WHAT THE CANAL IS GOING ON?

 Today in 2014 the Haresfoot Brewery in Berkhamsted shared an illustration on Facebook of a section of the Grand Union Canal that traverses the town, a colourful map showing local attractions surrounding the navigation. It was a perfectly nice, informative, inoffensive post. A short while later, a certain 'Paul Robbo Robinson' commented below it: 'It looks like a willy tee hee!!' This was childish, rude and, what's more, accurate. It did look like a willy, and once it had been pointed out everyone could see it. Somehow the story went viral and Berkhamsted was well and truly on the map. I bet Robbo is a Dad …

BEHAVE, BASIL

Some people seem to be able to get away with anything and even be rewarded for it. How about this for a charge list: shoplifting; indecent exposure and masochism; and insulting the Tsar. Dads get it in the neck for leaving the cap off the toothpaste, but when Basil, the so-called 'Holy Fool' of Moscow, did all these things, he was venerated. By robbing the rich to give to the poor, wandering round naked laden with chains and chiding Ivan the Terrible for his wicked ways, Basil ended up a saint. When he died today in 1552, Ivan even acted as a pallbearer.

QUICK, HIDE, HE'LL KILL YOU!

A warning to Dads not to be too overprotective of their daughters now. On this day in 1667 John Spencer was made master of Corpus Christi College, Cambridge, and took up residence with his wife and daughter Elizabeth.

As the only eligible female at college, Elizabeth was quite a distraction, and she soon had a dalliance with an undergraduate. One day they were together when she heard her father approaching, so she bundled him into a cupboard to hide. It was a tiny space, though, and by the time she could release him the poor lad had asphyxiated. Elizabeth threw herself from the roof with grief and guilt, and her ghost now haunts the college.

AUGUST

DRINKING THE STARS

Testimony to the fact that Dads will believe any old guff if it sounds good enough, today in 1693 French monk Dom Perignon invented champagne! As if there hadn't been fizzy alcoholic drinks knocking around for ages beforehand. Apparently Dom was trying to *get rid* of the bubbles from his wine, got fed up and decided to taste it, then announced, 'Come quickly, I am drinking the stars!' The earliest documented evidence for these words is from the 1880s from an unimpeachably even-handed source – a champagne ad.

TO BE A PILGRIM

Some of the most famous Dads in history are celebrated today – sort of. The Pilgrim Fathers set off today in 1620 from … Southampton. Hang on, I hear you ask, I thought they sailed from Plymouth. And so they did, eventually, in the *Mayflower* on 6 September. But first they set off in two ships from Southampton. One of them was the *Speedwell* (a very Dad-like name – it probably had go-faster stripes), which was such a leaky old hulk that it was quickly abandoned and everyone (well, most of them) piled onto the *Mayflower*. American land was first sighted by the colonists on 9 November.

ARACHNID AEROSOL EPIDEMIC

I blame the manufacturers, personally. Nowhere on any aerosol I have ever bought does it say *not* to use it to kill spiders. In 2010 Dad of two Chris Welding sprayed a spider with deodorant as it crouched behind a toilet – he then lit his lighter to see if it was dead. Result: serious burns to his torso. In July 2014 a Seattle chap used a spray paint and a lighter to improvise a flame-thrower. Result: $60,000 damage to his house. Finally, today in 2014 a man from Bridgend also went down the aerosol-lighter route. Result: a visit from the Welsh fire brigade. Seriously, Dads, just put your foot down.

I'M A BIT THOR!

Norwegian explorer Thor Heyerdahl was convinced that people from South America could have settled the Pacific Polynesian islands, so in April 1947 he set out from Peru on a balsa-wood raft with five companions to prove the voyage was possible in a simple craft. Today, after 101 days, the *Kon-Tiki* crashed into a reef in French Polynesia after a 6,984km (4,340 mile) journey – Thor had wrecked his boat but proved his point. They were rescued by locals after a few days and eventually *Kon-Tiki* was towed to Tahiti. Heyerdahl married three times and had several kids – only a Dad could hit a tiny reef in the middle of the world's largest ocean.

AUSTRALIAN SCOTSMAN

Mention classic steam engines to most Dads and one name will probably spring to mind: the *Flying Scotsman*. And yet before the name was given to a famous locomotive built in 1923, the 'Flying Scotsman' was the popular name used to refer to the 'Special Scotch Express', an express passenger service between Edinburgh and London that had been operating since 1862. The loco, designed by Nigel Gresley, went on to break the 100mph (160kph) barrier and remains a worldwide mechanical celebrity. Today in 1989 it set the world long-distance non-stop steam record in Australia by running for 679km (422 miles).

AGGERS GETS THE GIGGLES

Dads love a good double entendre, and on this day in 1991 came a standout moment when Jonathan Agnew and the late Brian Johnston were summarising the day's play in the Test against West Indies. Recalling the fall of Ian Botham's wicket – he had overbalanced and dislodged a bail despite his best efforts – Agnew remarked, 'He just didn't quite get his leg over.' He and Johnners then spent the next couple of minutes convulsed in snorts and giggles. Reportedly, they caused a 3.2km (2 mile) tailback at the Dartford Tunnel as listeners couldn't pay their tolls for laughing.

I DIDN'T RAC THE SIGNS, YOUR HONOUR

Any Dad who has ever been caught speeding might raise a glass (not while driving, obviously) to the Royal Automobile Club, founded today in 1897 with the aim of campaigning to raise the 'absurd' speed limit of 14mph (22kph). Just as important to founder members, it was a rather exclusive gentleman's club in Pall Mall, though it took it 10 years to earn its 'Royal' title. It also went on to organise motor races and in 1901 introduced its roadside assistance, invaluable to clueless motoring Dads. They won a major victory in 1903 when the new Motor Car Act raised the speed limit ... to 20mph (32kph).

WHAT'S HE SAID NOW?

What is it with American Presidents and Veeps and foot-in-mouth syndrome? Before Dan Quayle and George 'Dubya' Bush there was former B-movie actor Ronald Reagan, who today in 1984, while doing a sound check for his weekly radio broadcast, declared: 'I've signed legislation that will outlaw Russia forever. We begin bombing in five minutes.' This wouldn't have mattered so much had it not been recorded and later leaked, causing an international row. At least when Dads put their foot in it they don't nearly start World War Three.

FINISHED!

Today in 1093 the foundation stone for the wonderful Durham Cathedral was laid. The resulting building is now a World Heritage Site, magnificently sited on a promontory above the River Wear. Considering they had no JCBs and the scaffolding would have been rudimentary and perilous, the fact that it took only 40 years to complete was astonishing for the era. Mind you, can you imagine the reaction if a Dad took 40 years to build a garden shed? You'd expect it to win a few awards.

FAWN OF THE DEAD

Was that the working title for Walt Disney's fifth animated feature, which had its New York première today in 1942? There were a few tears in movie theatres when poor little Bambi's Mum was shot, but by the time the end credits rolled the antics of the white-tailed deer, and his cute mates Thumper and Flower, had cheered everyone up. The film, based on Felix Salten's novel *Bambi, A Life in the Woods*, won three Oscars and provided Dads with the cracking joke: What do you call a hunter that can shoot a deer with either hand? Bambidextrous!

WHAT AN ANTI-CLIMAX

More cricket now for Dads (well, it is summer), and another case of a player finding perfection just out of his reach (see 31 July). On this day in 1948, the great Don Bradman came out to bat against England in his final match. He needed four runs to average exactly 100 in Test cricket, a phenomenal feat. The crowd stood to applaud him to the wicket; the England team gave him three cheers. Then Eric Hollies bowled him second ball for a duck. 'The Don' trudged disconsolately off, and finished his career with a Test average of 99.94 – still nearly 40 runs per innings better than anyone else … but not quite Carling.

I'LL NAME THAT TUNE …

On this day in 1970 a tune was heard for the first time that would become the most recognisable TV theme tune in the UK (according to a 2010 survey). It might be old-fashioned, but hearing the opening trumpet strains of *Match of the Day* is enough to send any Dad into a reverie of his favourite matches from down the years. The tune, written by Barry Stoller, was given a revamp in the 1980s but there was such an uproar from viewers that the old brassy version was quickly restored and has survived ever since, becoming synonymous with football itself.

IT'LL NEVER CATCH ON (2)

Dads are either gadget-nuts or else notoriously late adopters of technology (usually the latter – it's cheaper) and many would have been wondering what they would use this new-fangled 'Internet Explorer' for when it was launched today in 1995 as part of Windows 95. I mean, you'd have to somehow connect your computer to your telephone line (meaning no one could call you), wait ages for pages of useless information to load one line at a time on your screen, then get disconnected and have to start all over again. This whole 'Internet' idea was obviously a non-starter.

WOULD I LIE TO YOU?

Dads must often feel like offering to take a lie-detector test to clear their name of some domestic misdemeanour – especially as there's little evidence that they work. Today in 1921 the *San Francisco Call and Post* reported the first use of John Larson's new polygraph machine in a criminal case. John Hightower was accused of the kidnap and murder of a priest, and the newspaper duly reported the test results sombrely and dispassionately: SCIENCE INDICATES HIGHTOWER'S GUILT! Fortunately for science (and justice), the police found plenty of other incriminating evidence, and Hightower spent the next 44 years in prison.

GIVE IT A REST!

Dads might think they work hard nowadays, but back in the 19th century the length of a working day depended on your employer's discretion. The seeds were planted for a significant victory for the proletariat on this day in 1855, when the Sydney Stonemasons' Society issued an ultimatum demanding an eight-hour day. They were in a strong position with a shortage of skilled labour, and a strike won concessions. A victory dinner was held on 1 October, a date now celebrated as Labor Day in New South Wales.

A POET IS BORN

Dads really only like poems when they're funny – limericks being their favourites (see 17 July). And one of the masters of humorous verse was born today in 1902 in Rye, New York State. Ogden Nash's wry rhymes have amused his fans since his first collection of verse was published in 1931, many of them animal-related – 'A wonderful bird is the pelican/Its beak can hold more than its bellican' – but he had more than a few words to say about being a Dad: 'Children aren't happy without something to ignore/And that's what parents were created for.'

TIME TO PROBE URANUS AGAIN

20 On this day in 1977 a space probe was launched by NASA to investigate the planets of our solar system and beyond. It passed Jupiter, Saturn and, in January 1986, Uranus. That was the last time we got close to this strange blue gas giant, but plans are afoot to return. Let's hope so. The butt of many Dad sniggers, this planet was discovered by William Herschel in 1781, so they let him name it. When he said he wanted to call it 'George's Star' (after King George III), fellow astronomers gave him the bum's rush and, luckily for infantile Dads everywhere, called it Uranus.

FINALLY, A FILM ABOUT US?

21 Today in 2009 a film was released that should have had Dads everywhere queuing up to see it. It was a comedy (a black one, but that's OK), it starred the late, great Robin Williams, it had good reviews, and finally it had the best title ever. – *World's Greatest Dad*. It turns out the title was a tad ironic (you'd have thought they could have warned us and used a question mark), with the Dad in question behaving in a very questionable way after the awkward death of his son. He ends the film by diving naked into the school swimming pool.

BLESS YOU!

22 Lots of Dads have funny hobbies, but very few to match Birmingham's Peter Fletcher. This Dad decided in July 2007 it would be a good idea to record every time he sneezed and log it online. By this day in 2014 he was up to 4,019 and was about to embark on an MSc in medical statistics. You can check out his fascinating records at sneezecount.joyfeed.com, where a typical entry reads, 'Coach B, 0733 to London, New St Station Moderate On way to Boring IV'. Personally I think he's a spy and this is the best 'cover' ever devised ...

SKYSPORTSIO!

23 Dads have always been grateful for the TV remote, that little gadget that saves them the effort of crossing the room to change channels. The first – the Flash-matic – was invented by Chicago-born Eugene Polley in 1955. But on this day in 2010 the device surely reached its zenith. The jaws of Britain's Dads dropped as they watched Richard Blakesley and Chris Barnardo make their pitch on BBC TV's *Dragons' Den* for investment in their magic wand that worked as a TV remote control. Unsurprisingly, they got their cash, and the wand remote can now be yours for just £49.95. Put it on your Christmas list, Dads.

SNACK ATTACK

24 Most Dads don't like to make a fuss, but they're glad one pernickety customer did on this day in Saratoga Springs in 1853. Having ordered fried potatoes at Moon's Lake House, the diner kept sending them back saying they were 'too thick'. Finally losing his temper, chef George Crum sliced a potato razor-thin, fried it and seasoned it with extra salt – the customer loved it and the potato crisp was born! So we have to thank the Americans, even though they still insist on calling them 'potato chips'. In the UK we chomp through six billion packets every year, with our favourite flavour being good old cheese and onion.

JAM TOMORROW? APPARENTLY NOT

25 We all love a good horror story, and a Dad's top nightmare is to be stuck in a traffic jam (especially if the car is full of kids). So when the *Daily Mail* reported on this day in 2010 that the 'Great Crawl of China', a 96-km (60 mile), 11-day tailback from Beijing to Inner Mongolia, 'could last a further three weeks', we settled down to enjoy a fortnight's coverage of motoring mayhem. But we were disappointed. By the time all the Western journalists turned up the following day, the traffic jam had more or less disappeared. The *Daily Mail* hyping a non-story, or a motoring miracle? You decide.

ISSIGONIS IS-A-GOOD'UN

When on this day in 1959 Alec Issigonis' Mark I Mini was announced to the world, few would have confidently predicted that this cute little car would become the icon of the Swinging Sixties. In 1999 this terrific little runabout was voted into second place in a 'Car of the Century' poll of 126 motor experts. As well as being the car many Dads learned to drive in, it also provides them with a series of awful jokes, beginning with: How do you get four elephants in a Mini? Two in the front, and two in the back!

'I THINK WE'LL JUST HAVE HIM CREMATED'

Today in 1963 saw the Broadway opening of a new show at the Morosco Theatre. *Oh Dad, Poor Dad* was a farce by Arthur L. Kopit that ran for 47 performances. A title role for the Dad sounds great; trouble is, he doesn't get that many lines because he's dead, and his widow has had him stuffed so he can accompany her wherever she goes – a bit of an extreme way to keep your eye on your hubby. The strange nature of the play is revealed in its full title: *Oh Dad, Poor Dad, Mamma's Hung You in the Closet and I'm Feelin' So Sad: A Pseudoclassical Tragifarce in a Bastard French Tradition.*

WHAT HAPPENED TO MY DAY OF REST?

A good and bad day for Dads in 1994, when Sunday trading in the UK was legalised. Smaller shops had been opening for years, with the law turning a blind eye, but now the big boys waded in, and soon Sunday would become just another day, and not great for Dads or Mums working in shops. Still, at least now Dads faced with an awkward task at home can 'nip out' for a couple of hours to the DIY superstore on the Sabbath to get that vital tool, which with any luck will be out of stock.

WHAT A RELIEF

Dads aren't great with buttons, especially on kids' clothes, so the more zippers on them the better. And the thought of going back to fumbling with button-fly trousers is a distressing one to any Dad who's been caught short with a full bladder. So hurray for Whitcomb L. Judson, who today in 1893 received a US patent for his 'clasp-locker' and the machine that made it. The clasp locker was the forerunner of the modern zip-fastener, although the name 'zipper' wasn't used until 1923. Now all we need is one guaranteed not to trap anything delicate on the way back up …

NO BUM NOTES, GUARANTEED

On this day in 1996 a historic step forward was taken in the quest for world peace when the first World Air Guitar Championships were held in the Finnish city of Oulu. Unsurprisingly the result was a Finnish 1-2-3, with Oikku Ylinen taking the inaugural prize of a Fender Stratocaster (not sure if it was any use to him or not). According to the founders, the competition was based on 'a peace ideology; a person playing the Air Guitar cannot simultaneously be up to any mischief'. No one can agree on who invented the air guitar or when, but it was probably a Dad desperate for an instrument he could play.

THE BOWLER WAS NASHING HIS TEETH

We've had two instances so far of cricketing near-perfection, so let's end the summer with someone who made it. Malcolm Nash was a medium-pace bowler for Glamorgan. Inspired by England wizard Derek Underwood, today in 1968 he decided to experiment with a bit of spin of his own. Unfortunately for him, he chose to do it against Nottinghamshire's Gary Sobers, one of the deadliest hitters in world cricket. Six balls later, each of which Sobers had despatched over the boundary, the experiment was over, and the West Indian had become the first cricketer to hit six sixes in an over.

SEPTEMBER

THIS OLD MAN

'My old man's a dustman,' sang Lonnie Donegan in 1960. 'My old man said follow the van,' warbled Marie Lloyd in the 1920s. Whether as parent or hubby, why should Dads have to put up with the indignity of being called 'my old man', and in derogatory contexts at that? Now, 'the old man' is quite different: they're always wise, like Prince Charles' 'The Old Man of Lochnagar'; impressive, like 'The Old Man of Coniston' in the Lake District; or gutsy and determined, like the fisherman in Ernest Hemingway's Pulitzer Prize-winning novel *The Old Man and the Sea*, published today in 1952. It's just not fair …

NOW THAT'S WHAT I CALL A LIE-IN!

In 46 BC Julius Caesar made the calendar of the Roman Empire more accurate by introducing the leap year every four years, and this Julian calendar was an improvement on its predecessors. But it still gained about three days every four centuries compared to the solar year, so by the end of the 16th century the spring equinox was about 11 days earlier than it should have been. Pope Gregory introduced a refined version in 1582, and the calendar was adjusted accordingly. It took Britain, still suspicious of Catholics, a few years to agree to fall in with this, but in 1752 hard-working Dads went to bed on 2 September and woke up on the 14th!

POETIC LICENCE

Whenever Dads are caught out in a slight misunderstanding over factual accuracy (i.e. making things up), they try to claim 'poetic' or 'artistic' licence. So it's good for them that they have one of the masters to rely on to back them up. William Wordsworth's *Poems, In Two Volumes*, includes the sonnet 'Composed upon Westminster Bridge, September 3, 1802' that begins, 'Earth hath not anything to show more fair'. Lovely. Except we know he crossed that bridge in a carriage on 31 July, at six o'clock in the morning ... I bet he was asleep.

WHO'S THE DADDY?

4 That was the battle-cry of Ulster strongman Glenn Ross in the 1990s and 2000s as he invariably led the British challenge in World's Strongest Man competitions. Although he never quite managed to break into the world's elite, he was Britain's/UK's strongest man eight times and on this day in 2004 won his best title, the European Masters Strongman Cup. At his peak he weighed in at 184kg (406lb) and was eating 8,000 calories every day. Sounds like your typical Dad, then, except that instead of lounging on sofas he was lifting them.

SUNNY JIM'S SONG AND DANCE

5 Dads are always bursting into song at the most inappropriate moment – singing 'Just One Cornetto' to the ice-cream man is a favourite – so it was fun today in 1978 when the Prime Minister got in on the act. James Callaghan was addressing the TUC conference in Brighton; the whole nation was expecting him to announce an imminent general election. Incredibly, instead of speaking, 'Sunny Jim' started singing: 'There was I, waiting at the church …' He couldn't be stopped, and finished a whole verse of the famous music-hall song before everyone realised there wouldn't be an election until the following year. He lost.

WILLIAM ISN'T TELLING

Dads, definitely don't try this one at home, you'll never get the blood out of the carpet. Today in 1953 William Burroughs, Beat Generation novelist and most famous for his *Naked Lunch* in 1959, was playing a drunken game with his wife Joan Vollmer. She balanced a glass of water on her head, he aimed his gun at it *à la* William Tell. Both were drunk and/or drugged-up. Joan might not have been expecting him to pull the trigger; maybe Burroughs never meant to. The gun went off, Joan was shot through the head, and a lucky Burroughs was only convicted of manslaughter.

DON'T MAKE ME TAKE THE OATH T-T-T-TWICE

It's a shame we've lost the knack of giving pithy nicknames to kings and queens and just go on boringly numbering them. It would be much more fun if Victoria the Fat had been succeeded by Edward the Randy, for instance. They knew how to do it back in ninth-century France, when Louis had Charles the Bald for a Dad (poor old Dad) and Charles the Simple for a son. Unsurprisingly, Louis the Stammerer was a nervous type who was crowned King of France twice, the second time today in 878. After giving away some of his land to Wilfred the Hairy, he died in 879.

TIME TO FIND ANOTHER CLICHÉ

Dads, are you fed up of being told you're about as much use as a chocolate teapot? Well, any Dad watching BBC's *The One Show* (OK, it's a long shot, but stay with me) today in 2014 would have been punching the air as they watched the world's first such working model being put through its paces. Developed in York by Nestlé's Product Technology Centre, it was made by building up layer after layer of special dark choccy using a silicon mould, and delivered a cuppa that was described as being 'a lovely cup of tea' with (guess what?) 'a slight hint of chocolate'.

A BUG'S LIFE

It's no wonder Dads can't get on with computers when there are so many bugs in them. The very first one was discovered today in 1947 when Grace Hopper, a US Navy scientist, was working on the Harvard Mark II, a very early model. She had to remove a dead moth that was stuck between the relays of the machine, and noted in the log book, 'First actual case of a bug being found'. 'Amazing Grace' went on to become not only a rear admiral, but a pioneering figure in computing history, showered with awards and honours.

SEPTEMBER

THAT'LL DO NICELY

The introduction of credit cards to Britain was a boon to cash-strapped Dads, but the fee on one of the first ones was a bit steep when it was launched on this day in 1963. At £3 12s (£3.60) per year, the new American Express card was aimed at 'managers and sales executives earning £2,000 a year or more' – in other words, top dollar. It reminds me of the chap who, when asked if he'd reported his stolen credit card yet, replied, 'No, the thief's spending less on it than my wife did!'

COMIC-BOOK HERO

Today in 1954, when the new comic *Tiger* hit the shops, it contained a character who became so famous a cliché bears his name – any implausibly impressive football feat will inevitably be dubbed 'real Roy of the Rovers stuff'. Dads dream of emulating Roy Race, and the Melchester star had quite a career: winning numerous trophies, enjoying foreign tours (on most of which he would be kidnapped) and surviving a murder attempt before his playing career was ended when he lost a leg in a helicopter crash. His comic strip last appeared in *Match of the Day* magazine in 2001, but in October 2014 he bounced back with the publication of his 'official autobiography'.

A MAMMOTH TASK

Proof that even Palaeolithic Dads couldn't help themselves from doodling whenever they had a spare moment was discovered today in 1940 in Lascaux in the Dordogne area of France. An 18-year-old stumbled on the entrance to a cave, and further exploration revealed nearly 2,000 cave paintings – animals, humans and abstract figures – estimated to be around 17,000 years old. The caves were opened to the public after the war, but closed in 1963, because the humidity produced by visitors was damaging the paintings. Scientists are still trying to work out how best to preserve these early artworks – even preservationists are allowed in for only very short periods.

MATT MAKES AN EXHIBITION OF HIMSELF

Dads like to think they're funny; they're usually wrong, but they know a witty chap when they see one. And for the last 25 years or so, no one has tickled the funny bone quite like Matthew Pritchett – known simply as 'Matt' – pocket cartoonist for *The Daily Telegraph*. Son of humorous columnist Oliver Pritchett, and grandson of writer V.S. Pritchett, Matt has been Cartoonist of the Year five times, received the MBE in 2002, and today in 2014 an exhibition of his work opened at the National Trust's Nunnington Hall, North Yorkshire.

DAD DANCING!

What a relief for US Dads today in 1960 when a record finally hit number one that they could dance to. No worrying whether you should put your left foot forward with your left arm, or how quickly you should shimmy. You just planted your feet on the floor and twisted up and down for 2 minutes 34 seconds, then when Chubby Checker had finished singing 'The Twist' you staggered off to A&E to have your knees done. Far from being a one-trick pony, Chubby followed this up with 'Let's Twist Again', 'Slow Twistin'' and 'Twist It Up'.

A THOUSAND PRANCING HORSES

Well, nearly. Race days are a popular special present for Dads nowadays, but one turning up at Silverstone today in 2012 would have had to bring his own very special vehicle, as 964 Ferraris filled the track to shatter the Guinness World Record for the largest parade of the classic Italian car. F1 star Felipe Massa led the procession in a 458 Spider as an estimated £80m of motors took part, raising thousands of pounds for automotive charity BEN.

TINSLEY'S TEA-TIME TREASURE

16 The only thing Dads love more than a nice cuppa is a nice cuppa with a digestive to dunk in it. Only trouble is, half the time we can't resist over-dunking. Result: a tea full of soggy biccy. What fantastic news reported in the *Daily Mail* today in 2014, then, that Dad of two (naturally) Andrew Tinsley had invented a simple mesh device to place in the pre-dunked mug that catches any deviant digestives that fall off. These can be removed to leave an untainted cuppa. The 'Cookie Catcher' is washable and reusable, and a snip at just £2.

WRIGHT PILOT, WRONG PASSENGER

17 Aeroplanes are a lot safer than nervous Dads think (see 6 July). Considering the first powered heavier-than-air flight was made in December 1903, it's a miracle that it was nearly five years before the first fatality in a plane crash. Lieutenant Tom Selfridge of the US Army was an aviation enthusiast and early military pilot. Today in 1908 he went up as a passenger with Orville Wright at Fort Myer, but a broken propeller caused a heavy nose-first landing. Wright was badly injured and Selfridge was killed – a flying helmet would probably have saved him.

PALMER'S PATRICIDE?

Daniel David Palmer was a beekeeper, schoolteacher, storekeeper and magnetic healer. He claimed divine inspiration and that he'd discovered the answer to the question, 'What is life?' Today in 1895 he examined a deaf janitor from Davenport, Iowa, with a back complaint. Palmer manipulated his spine, curing his lumbago and his deafness simultaneously and inventing chiropractic treatment. He set up a school to train others, which he eventually sold to his son, B.J. They fell out and in 1913, according to some accounts, B.J. deliberately ran over his Dad with a car, resulting in his death.

LIGHTS! CAMERAS! SICK BUCKET!

Although this will send a shiver down the spines of some Dads as they recall crawling along in a traffic jam on the promenade, with a collection of travel-sick infants throwing up in the back seat, many will have fond memories of Blackpool Illuminations, which were switched on for the first time on this day in 1879. Just eight arc lights illuminated the prom on that first night – now they use over a million. Among the celebrities who have switched on the lights are Ken Dodd, Kermit the Frog and Red Rum.

'I'M SURE HE WON'T MIND A BIT OF RAIN'

The Great Buddha of Kamakura is an enormous (13m [43ft]) bronze statue dating from the 13th century that stands in the open air in all its glory in the Kanagawa Prefecture of Japan. It was originally protected by a hall; when this was destroyed by a storm in 1334, it was rebuilt; another storm in 1369 damaged the hall again, and again it was rebuilt. When this building was washed away in a tsunami today in 1498, a Japanese Dad who just wanted a lie-down suggested that maybe Buddha was trying to tell them something, and the statue's been exposed to the elements ever since.

SO, IS THERE A SANTA CLAUS?

This is a frequent question asked of Dads, but as you get older you realise just how stupid it is. Of course there's a Santa Claus. Today in 1897 *The New York Sun* printed an editorial in reply to a letter from eight-year-old Virginia O'Hanlon asking just that question, and it has gone down in US history, spawning a book, a TV movie, charity campaigns and even a cantata. Editor Francis Church pointed out that just because you can't see something – like love and generosity – doesn't mean it's not there, and reminded everybody how 'dreary' the world would be without Santa. Well said, Francis.

SEPTEMBER

IS THERE ANYTHING ON THE OTHER SIDE?

Before this day in 1955, this was a question that would never be asked by a UK telly-watcher. Up until then there was only one BBC channel. Then commercial television arrived to shake things up, and 12 minutes later Dads in London (where ITV launched) were already grinding their teeth as the first TV advert was screened, appropriately for Gibbs SR toothpaste. The sneaky Beeb had tried to undermine ITV's big day with a tragic disaster episode of popular radio soap *The Archers*, but multi-channel telly was here to stay.

HOUSTON? IT'S ABOUT 3 FEET AND 14 CENTIMETRES ...

Dads are prone to getting in a muddle over metric, particularly the older ones who remember pounds, shillings and pence (see 15 February). So it was reassuring today in 1999 when NASA's Mars Climate Observer burned up over the red planet after getting its trajectory wrong while being placed into orbit. After a couple of months, red-faced officials announced the cause of the $193m mishap. One piece of software had been programmed in imperial and had passed results to another program that was expecting them in metric. Oops!

STAFFORDSHIRE GOLD RUSH

Dads know just what it's like to put something down for a minute and then forget where it is. So it was probably a Dad who was wandering around Mercia about 1,400 years ago, popped his stash of gold into a handy hole in the ground then couldn't find it again. It resurfaced again in July 2009, in a field near Lichfield, and on 24 September the discovery of the largest hoard of Anglo-Saxon gold and silver ever was announced. It was declared 'treasure trove', and thus the property of the Crown, but detectorist Terry Herbert and field-owner Fred Johnson still shared £3.2m when the historic find was acquired jointly by museums in Birmingham and Stoke.

DAD, YOU'RE ON TELLY

On this day in 1997 a BBC sitcom began that Dads could look at and think, 'That programme's got my name on it.' *Dad* concerned the tribulations of middle-aged Alan and his Dad Brian, played by George Cole. In a role that was a far cry from his wheeler-dealer Arthur Daley days, Cole's character constantly exasperates his son; sounds about right for a Dad. Though never a massive hit, it went to a second series and is described by the British Comedy Guide website as 'deceptively dark' and 'on the whole … good'. I think most Dads would settle for a crit like that.

SOUNDS PAINFUL

26 I know we've already encountered Sir Francis Drake on 4 April, but on this day in 1580 he sailed into Plymouth on the *Golden Hind* with a hold full of treasure. Elizabeth I's half-share exceeded the rest of her income for the entire year and, more importantly for us, Drake became the first Englishman to circumnavigate the globe. This little nugget of information has been mangled by pupils down the years and appears regularly in those collections of schoolboy howlers so beloved of Dads as: 'Francis Drake circumcised the world with a 100-foot clipper.'

WHO WANTS TO BE A MILLIONAIRE?

 **27** It was a good job for little orphan Annie that Oliver 'Daddy' Warbucks did, because in Harold Gray's comic strip the benevolent businessman was always helping out Annie when she was in trouble. Lacking children of his own, he took a special interest in the adventures of the ~~annoying~~ adorable youngster. His character appeared for the first time today in 1924, a few weeks after the strip's debut in the New York *Daily News*. The strip was turned into a hit musical in 1977.

SEE, *THAT'S* WHY I DON'T WASH UP

There's such a thing as being too tidy. On 3 September 1928 scientist Alexander Fleming went on holiday without washing up in his laboratory. He had a four-year-old son, so he had his priorities right. When he got back on 28 September he noticed a Petri dish with some mould growing in it. Presumably in an attempt to delay cleaning up still further, Fleming had a good look at the mould, which seemed to have killed the surrounding staphylococci culture. *Et voilà!* Penicillin was discovered.

MYSTERY AT SEA

Dads love a good whodunit, and when Rudolf Diesel, inventor of the diesel engine (there are a few Dads out there still amazed at that coincidence), disappeared from his cabin on the steamer *Dresden* in the English Channel today in 1913 it had all the ingredients. His bed was unslept in and his nightshirt was laid out. His hat and overcoat were found by the ship's railing. His body was found by Dutch fishermen 10 days later, but it was so decomposed they removed his effects and returned it to the sea. So did he jump or was he pushed? Well, he did have money troubles, but he was also travelling to England to discuss making his engines available to British submarines … on the eve of World War One.

LIVENS CLEANS UP

On this day in 1914 a certain William Howard Livens was enrolled in the British Army as a Second Lieutenant. This inventor was more crack-shot than crackpot (he was a champion marksman) and was definitely the sort of chap you'd want on your side, as he devised ingenious ways of delivering death and destruction to the enemy, principally via gas bombs and flamethrowers. But all that was the prelude to his greatest hour, when in 1924 he invented the first domestic dishwasher, meaning that no longer would Dads have to break all the best china in an effort to get out of washing up.

OCTOBER

ARE YOU SMARTER THAN A
10-YEAR-OLD?

Attention, Dads. Today in 1946 a Very Important Organisation was formed: it was exclusive, elitist and educated. So I won't waste time telling you about Mensa, which welcomes only those in the top 2 per cent of IQ. You need to know about Densa, an open, informal grouping for the other 94 per cent of us who can't add up or spel. Various versions have been knocking around since the 1970s, and you can even buy T-shirts online to show off your status. Prospective members will need to answer searching questions such as 'Who wrote Handel's *Messiah*?' and 'Is it legal to marry your widow's sister?'

WORKING FOR PEANUTS FOR 50 YEARS

A chap who constantly feels the world is against him, has no hair and is always being put in his place by a confident, self-assured female. No wonder Dads associate so much with Charlie Brown, who first appeared in the debut *Peanuts* comic strip today in 1950. 'Most of us are much more acquainted with losing than winning,' was creator Charles M. Schulz's explanation. The classic cartoon, which was as much about philosophy as comedy, ran for nearly 50 years before the final strip – announcing the end of *Peanuts* – was published on 13 February 2000. Sadly Schulz never got to enjoy his retirement – he died the day before.

THOSE WERE THE DAYS ...

In 1949 a radio programme began in the USA whose title epitomised the spirit of the times. *Father Knows Best* was a popular comedy starring Robert Young as Dad-of-three Jim Anderson; it transferred to TV today in 1954. Young continued as Jim, and this utterly believable, inspiring story of a 'thoughtful father who offered sage advice' to his children ran until 1960. Then the permissive society arrived and kids started making their own decisions – bloomin' cheek.

A MOVING MOMENT

It's hard work lugging small kids' paraphernalia up and down stairs, so what a great day for Dads today in 1911 when Britain's first underground-station escalator was demonstrated at Earl's Court. The public were suspicious, so a chap with one leg called Bumper Harris (I don't know what his other leg was called!) was employed to ride it all day to show how safe it was. Britain's first escalator had been installed in 1898 at Harrods, but despite the free brandy on offer at the top to calm people down after the ascent, it was not the sort of place to find your average Dad.

I WISH TO REGISTER A COMPLAINT

Monty Python's Flying Circus is probably one of those shows that separates the Dads from the Granddads. For many older Dads in the late 1960s, the ones who probably thought *The Goons* were dangerously subversive, they couldn't understand why anyone would find it funny. For the rest of us, though we couldn't explain why, it was often hilarious, despite (or perhaps because) of being 'silly', as Graham Chapman's Colonel would say. It all began on this day in 1969, and in 2014 the pensioner Pythons were packing in the crowds at London's O2 Arena.

I DO, I DO, I DO

In the latter half of the 19th century the Church of Jesus Christ of Latter-Day Saints – the Mormons to me and you – were having trouble juggling their practice on polygamy (as laid down by founder Joseph Smith in the 1830s) with US law and popular opinion. Fortunately, as the political pressure mounted, Mormon leader Wilford Woodruff received a personal instruction from Jesus that the policy should change, and today in 1890 their 'Manifesto' officially made it one wife per husband. And all Dads know what the maximum sentence for bigamy is – two mothers-in-law!

WE WERE LUCKY TO GET NIL

Most Dads will be familiar with the experience of witnessing their child's school team being utterly humiliated in a sporting event, usually in the pouring rain, and having to utter meaningless words of consolation afterwards, when what they really want to say is, 'Can't you at least find an *indoor* sport to be useless at?' So spare a thought for anyone who had a son playing for Cumberland College today in 1916 when they lost 222–0 to Georgia Tech at American football. Cumberland's coach was George Allen – probably a distant relation …

FAST FOOD ARRIVES

Perhaps the most famous example of a serendipitous discovery is Fleming forgetting to wash up his Petri-dishes and finding Penicillin (see 28 September). But a much more useful invention for impatient Dads was also the result of a happy accident. When in 1945 American Percy Spencer was experimenting with microwaves and realised a chocolate bar had melted in his pocket, his first thought was to verify his theory by making some popcorn. Later that year, on this day, his company Raytheon filed a patent application for the world's first microwave oven.

DOES MY BUM LOOK BIG IN THIS?

Dads aren't always the most svelte of God's creatures, so it was uplifting today in 1991 for them to see specimens of manhood that made most of them look distinctly skinny as the Royal Albert Hall hosted the first sumo tournament to be held outside Japan in the sport's 1,500-year history. The five-day basho saw 40 wrestlers descend on London including the heaviest sumo wrestler ever, the 238kg (525lb) Konishiki (nicknamed the Dump Truck, later in his career he would hit 287kg (633lb). The Royal Garden Hotel prepared for his and the others' visit by weight-testing the toilets and reinforcing the furniture.

HANDBALL, REF!

It's very tricky controlling a ball with only your feet, as many Dads know from experience. It is far easier, and very tempting, to just pick the ball up and run with it – and that, supposedly, is exactly what William Webb Ellis did at Rugby School one day in 1823, laying the foundations for the game of rugby union. This (probably mythical) event was first described on this day in 1876 (four years after Webb Ellis's death, conveniently) when another former Rugby scholar wrote to *The Meteor*, the school magazine. Rugby – a game played by men with funny-shaped balls – has embraced the legend enthusiastically.

NOT TO BE CONFUSED WITH WOOLLOOMOOLOO

Today in 1852 Australian Dads could aspire for their sons (and, 30 years later, daughters) to go to a real university, when Sydney University was inaugurated. It now regularly ranks among the top 50 in the world, has nearly 50,000 students and in the 1960s had *two* thriving philosophy departments, when there was a split after an academic spat. Unlike the famous Monty Python 'Bruces' sketch, we don't know which ended up in charge of logical positivism and which was in charge of the sheep dip.

DO YOU HAVE A CRIMINAL RECORD, SIR?

Continuing the Aussie theme, today in 1867 the *Hougoumont* set sail from Portsmouth with 280 convicts on board, arriving at Fremantle, Australia, on 9 January 1868. They were the last of more than 165,000 criminals who had been shipped to Australia in the 80 years since the 'First Fleet' sailed in 1787. An estimated five million Australians are descended from convicts, about 20 per cent of the population. And a typical Dad's answer if asked the question in the title by Australian immigration control? 'I didn't know you still needed one!'

DAY OF DELIGHT

When a cave-in trapped 33 men 700m (2,300ft) underground at the San José copper-gold mine in Chile on 5 August 2010, it looked grim for them, especially when nothing was heard for 16 days. But on 22 August the miners managed to attach a note to an exploratory drill that had broken into their chamber, and the rescue proper could begin. It was still a long, risky and tortuous task to drill a hole large enough for escape, but today, after a record 69 days underground, all 33 were brought to the surface over a 22-hour period. One man even became a Dad while trapped, and watched his daughter being delivered via a video link!

I CAN'T BEAR IT!

What is it with brilliant authors calling their sons Christopher? There's Christopher Awdry (see 19 April), Christopher Tolkien, and ... well, modesty forbids me to go on. And then there is probably the most famous of them all, Christopher Robin Milne – yes, the son of Winnie the Pooh creator A.A. Milne, whose name was made famous by the little bear's friend in the stories. The first collection was published today in 1926 and was soon a publishing hit. It was educational too – in 1960 a Latin version (*Winnie ille Pu*) became the first foreign-language book to feature in the *New York Times* bestsellers list.

FUNKY MONKEY BOOK

Near to the top of all Dad lists of 'books I ought to read but never will' is surely Edward Gibbon's six-volume *The History of the Decline and Fall of the Roman Empire*. Epic in scope, with a magisterial title, the abridged version only runs to 850 pages so is perfectly knock-offable for the average Dad in ... well, maybe not. Gibbon was supposedly inspired to write it when he heard Franciscan friars singing Vespers in Rome today in 1764. The work's title has been borrowed or adapted many times, most notably by Evelyn Waugh in 1928.

WHAT A WAY TO GO

16 OK, this is a rather tasteless entry, but hopefully the passing of 200 years since the event means the London Beer Flood of 1814 can be remembered without too much sober reflection. After all, we all have to die sometime, and there are surely worse ways than drowning in beer. When a huge vat containing 135,000 gallons of liquid heaven burst at the Meux & Co Brewery on Tottenham Court Road, London, at least eight people were killed. The situation wasn't helped by some people dashing to the scene to scoop up the ale rather than help with the rescue. A court later ruled the deluge was an 'Act of God', meaning no one was held responsible.

FORE!

17 While many of us would agree with Mark Twain that it's 'a good walk spoiled' or G.K. Chesterton that it's 'an expensive way of playing marbles', there's no doubt that when some Dads get bitten by the golf bug they can't shake it off. The very first Open Golf Championship was played today in 1860 when eight men played three rounds in a single day at Prestwick in Scotland. There was a home winner in Willie Park Snr, which was hardly surprising – it would be 30 years before the first non-Scottish Open Champion!

POP-UP PERFECTION

A nice cup of tea (see 10 January) is all very well, but it's a bit … well, wet without a round of toast to go with it. The problem with toast is that absent-minded Dads are prone to wandering off while it's under the grill, resulting in burned toast at best and a visit from the fire brigade at worst. So it was great news when Iowan Charles Strite received his patent for an automatic pop-up toaster on this day in 1921. Now all we needed was a way of making sure the bread was evenly sliced (see 7 July).

DAD, WHAT'S A VIDEO?

Don't you feel old when you remember the opening of the first Blockbuster video rental store, today in 1985 in Dallas? Before you could say 'chewed tape' the franchise had spread worldwide, with more than 9,000 stores. Sadly it couldn't keep up with modern trends, firstly people who like owning DVDs to watch multiple times, and then with new streaming on-demand services such as Netflix. There are a few stores left using the name, but Dads had better use up their old jokes soon before no one understands them: 'Can I rent *Batman Forever*?' 'No, you have to bring it back next week.'

OCTOBER
WHY ARE PIRATES SO SEXY?

Just because they arrrr! – as any Dad can tell you. And one of the most alluring of them all was 'Calico Jack' Rackham, a buccaneer in the Caribbean in the early 18th century. He designed the famous 'Jolly Roger' flag with the skull and crossed swords, and had two female crew members, Mary Read and his lover Anne Bonny. For a brief time he went straight, accepting an amnesty, but he couldn't resist piracy and returned to his old ways. He was captured today in 1720 and hanged a month later in Port Royal, Jamaica.

UP THE WORKERS!

There are left-wing Dads and right-wing Dads and, most of all, can't-stand-any-of-'em Dads, but they would all have been cheering on a strike called today in Egypt in 2007. The nation's tax-collectors, fed up of being badly paid, walked out today and stayed out for over a month. On 3 December they escalated their action to a sit-in outside the Ministers' Council building, which lasted for another 10 days. In desperation, the Council offered them a 325 per cent pay increase with a two-month bonus, the strikers happily went home and Egyptians had to pay their tax again.

EVERY HOME SHOULD HAVE ONE

On this day in 2013 US company Picobrew reached its target on the crowdfunding website Kickstarter, meaning production could get going on its innovative product, the Zymatic® home-brewing machine. Brothers Bill and Jim Mitchell spent three years developing the product. All the home brewer has to do is add water, hops and grain to the machine, choose a recipe, and set it going for a few hours. After adding yeast and waiting for another week, the 'high-quality craft beer' is ready. At 20 pints in a batch, and a cost of around £1,000, your first pint has only cost you about 50 quid.

HAPPY BIRTHDAY, WORLD!

If you're the patient sort who is savouring this book one day at a time, then assuming you're reading this today in 2015, I can inform you that the world is exactly 6,018* years old today (we Dads like to keep things precise). Anyway, that's according to Bishop James Ussher, Primate of All Ireland from 1625–56, who took it upon himself to calculate when God created the Earth. After going through all the begettings of the Old Testament and other ancient texts, he took a few educated guesses and came up with 23 October 4004 BC.

*If you're wondering why it isn't 6,019 – there was no year 0.

SUPERSONIC SCRAPHEAP

Concorde was such an icon of the 1970s it's hard to believe it will never fly again. Even more bewildering than the impressive 480kph (300mph) speed it crossed the Atlantic at was the fact that it was a successful (technologically speaking) Anglo-French project. As a money-making venture, however, it never took off, and only 20 were built. Today in 2003 British Airways retired its fleet, and misty-eyed Dads can now only regale their kids with tales of sonic booms of long ago.

JUST PUT HIM IN THE CORNER

You might be a Dad to two or three kids, or even five or six. But imagine what it must be like to be the father of hundreds of thousands, perhaps millions, of books – a relief that they don't need their nappies changing for a start. Geoffrey Chaucer is the man regarded as the father of English literature; his epic *Canterbury Tales* still influences writers today. On this day in 1400 he died and he was buried in Westminster Abbey because he was a tenant of the Abbey's close. In 1556 his remains were moved to a more ornate tomb in the area that would become known as Poets' Corner.

DULL OLD MAN IS NUTTER, I CONCLUDE

In 1991 the first World Memory Championship was held and was won by Dominic O'Brien, who managed to remember more random numbers, playing cards and other useless information than anybody else. This does not impress Dads, obviously, who see memory as an overrated virtue, but Dominic and his chums do utilise mnemonics an awful lot, and they can be a useful way to bore the kids. From the musical (Eddy Ate Dynamite, Good Bye Eddy – guitar strings) to tricky spellings (Dashing In A Rush, Running Harder Or Else Accident!), there's one for every use imaginable.

YOU'RE HAVING A LAUGH!

Most Dads mistakenly think of themselves as being naturally funny, but on this day in 1985 the Comedy Store Players performed their first improvised gig at London's Comedy Store (there's a coincidence), and nearly 30 years later they're still going strong, performing twice weekly. Paul Merton and Neil Mullarkey remain from the first-night line-up, but several others, such as Josie Lawrence and Richard Vranch, are long-standing contributors. Many of its members became well known on Channel 4's *Whose Line Is It Anyway?*, an improv format that has been much imitated (especially by Dads) but rarely bettered.

TELL IT TO THE MARINES

If your Dad tells you he was in the marines and you suspect he's telling porkies, why don't you tell him to 'Tell it to the marines': the phrase, dating back to at least 1804, originally continued '... because the sailors won't believe you', and implied a lack of trust. Nowadays the phrase has more martial connotations, as befitting a service whose origins go back to this day in 1664 with the founding of 'the Duke of York and Albany's maritime regiment of foot'. Their motto is *Per Mare Per Terram* – 'By sea, by land'.

STAND BY YOUR SON

In 1946 Terence Rattigan's play *The Winslow Boy* was first staged. It tells the inspiring story of a young boy wrongly accused of theft and expelled from school, whose father risks everything to clear his name. Based on the true 1908 expulsion of George Archer-Shee from Osborne Naval College, the play has twice been made into a film: Anthony Asquith's 1948 version, and in 1999, starring Nigel Hawthorne.

HANG ON WHILE I GRAB A LOUD ...

A loud what, though? Well, just a loud. If John J. Loud had got his act together after this day in 1888, when the first ballpoint pen was patented, we might never have heard of Laszlo Biro. Loud's device utilised a small rotating steel ball and was useful for marking coarse material like wood or leather. He couldn't get it fine enough for paperwork, though, and the patent lapsed. Technological problems plagued would-be imitators and it wasn't until the 1930s that something like the modern biro was produced, and Dads could throw away their blotting paper and write legibly; trouble is, now people could read their writing, it showed up their terrible spelling!

I'M SORRY, I'LL READ THAT AGAIN

Dads like it when someone else fouls things up – it takes the attention away from them. So they would have loved the story on BBC News online today in 2008. Swansea council emailed its in-house translation service requesting the Welsh for 'No entry for heavy goods vehicles. Residential site only.' They received a reply straight away, and lost no time in getting the bilingual sign produced. Before long, Welsh speakers were wondering why someone had erected a notice in their street that read: 'I am not in the office at the moment. Send any work to be translated.'

NOVEMBER

WRITING ON THE WALL FOR DADS

The first signs that Dads could become superfluous and hence an endangered species were revealed as far back as today in 1939, when the first artificially inseminated rabbit was introduced to the world by scientists. You'd have thought rabbits would be the last species that needed a helping hand to reproduce. The technique is now widespread in farming and has helped many women to conceive. At least AI still needs a male input – when Dolly the cloned sheep was unveiled in 1996, it hinted at a future where even that would be unnecessary.

THE PERMISSIVE SOCIETY

Dads are still divided over whether it was a good or bad thing, but if Philip Larkin was right in 'Annus Mirabilis', sexual intercourse began sometime between today in 1960 and July 1963 (the Beatles' first EP), and without that we'd have no Dads at all – I'm not sure what we did before then. Anyway, the verdict was brought in today in the famous *Lady Chatterley* obscenity trial, and Penguin Books was told it could publish D.H. Lawrence's ~~mucky book~~ literary masterpiece, even at the risk of one's wife or servants picking it up and leafing through it!

MAYDAY, I MEAN CQD, ER, HELP!

The invention of radio telegraphy in the late 19th century was a boon for shipping, as it meant they could keep in touch with other vessels and land stations within range. But until this day in 1906, no one could agree on what to signal if you were in trouble. 'HELP' was the first distress call made, but not much use if the recipient didn't speak English. 'CQD' was an early alternative ('*sécu*' from the French *sécurité*), but wasn't very snappy. Then at a Berlin conference in 1906 the famous dot-dot-dot, dash-dash-dash, dot-dot-dot we are all familiar with was adopted. Finally, a signal even the dopiest Dad could remember ... SOS.

DR DODD'S DEGREE

Next time Dad tells you that you won't get anywhere joking around, just refer him to Ken Dodd. The record-breaking (1,500 jokes in 3½ hours) gagster from Knotty Ash has been around the British comedy scene for as long as anyone can remember. Famous for his late-running shows that still regularly finish after midnight even now he's in his eighties, he's had hit records, received the OBE and even beat the taxman in a famous tax evasion case in 1989. And today in 2009 he received an honorary doctorate from Chester University.

ACE OF SPIES

Dads love a good spy story, and no one was more exciting and mysterious than Sidney Reilly. His life was a complex web of misdirection and exaggeration: did he murder his lover's husband? Did he steal Russian Navy plans and a secret German aviation component? Did he sell arms to both sides in World War One? The more you delve the murkier the waters get. We think we know that this man who might or might not have inspired Ian Fleming's creation of James Bond was executed today in 1925 by the Soviet secret police ... although some people insist it was a cover to hide his defection!

PERMISSION TO TWEAK, SIR?

This is not the sort of book that likes to celebrate deaths, but when it's at the end of a long, successful life we'll make an exception – especially when the person in question nearly died in childhood when an operation to remove a third nipple went wrong. Clive Dunn was only 48 when he was cast as octogenarian butcher Corporal Jones in *Dads' Army*, but his convincing war stories meant we could hardly believe he'd still been alive in 2012 when he died today at the age of 92. He probably slipped St Peter a pound of sausages to let him through the Pearly Gates.

IT'S JUST NOT CRICKET (2)

For decades and decades international cricket had got along just fine without neutral umpires – umpires couldn't be biased, it wasn't in the spirit of the game, you know. But in the 1970s and '80s growing professionalism meant stakes were higher and suspicions that some home umpires were favouring their own teams caused tempers to fray. On this day in 1986, Indian umpires stood in a Test match between Pakistan and West Indies at the invitation of Pakistan captain Imran Khan. Nowadays, every Test has neutral umpires, which gives Dads an excuse to get out of officiating at their kids' matches, citing 'international precedent'.

BREAKING NEWS

Kids are always falling off bikes and out of trees, but how's a Dad meant to tell the difference between a bruise and a break? It doesn't look good when we tell little Johnny to 'run it off' when it turns out he's fractured his ankle. Luckily, today in 1895 Wilhelm Röntgen discovered X-rays by accident while experimenting with cathode rays, leading to him winning the first Nobel Prize for physics. The first X-ray of a human body part was of his wife's hand; when she saw the bony image she apparently remarked: 'I have seen my own death.'

DON'T PANIC!

This is always good advice for Dads, even though it's normally transmitted in ways guaranteed to instil terror, such as Corporal Jones' gibbering entreaties in *Dads' Army* and on the cover of *The Hitchhikers' Guide to the Galaxy*. Today in 1979 the US early-warning system sprang into life, signalling that a nuclear strike was imminent. Interceptor planes were scrambled, the President's 'doomsday plane' was prepared and US missile systems were readied to retaliate. Then someone who hadn't panicked checked the satellite data, which showed nothing; a technician had accidentally loaded a training program that simulated a Russian attack. That was close!

LOST AND FOUND

It was a big day for Henry Morton Stanley in 1871 when he found explorer David Livingstone near Lake Tanganyika in what is now Tanzania. It wasn't such a big day for Livingstone because he hadn't realised he was lost. Welshman Stanley was a journalist commissioned by the *New York Herald* to find the Scottish missionary, who hadn't been heard of for some time. Whether his famous greeting, 'Dr Livingstone, I presume?' was fact, or a good line dreamed up afterwards, is unclear. Dads, of course, are no stranger to getting lost, but oddly no one ever sends out search parties for them ...

GET YOUR KICKS

When Dads have their obligatory midlife crisis they often dream of freewheeling along an open highway in the US, and are drawn naturally to Route 66, immortalised by myriad songsters including Nat King Cole and Chuck Berry. Connecting Chicago to Santa Monica and stretching nearly 4,000km (2,500 miles), it was established today in 1926 as one of the original highways of the US auto system, and is also referred to as the 'Mother Road' and the 'Will Rogers Highway' – though 'I got my kicks on the Will Rogers Highway' doesn't have quite the same ring to it.

NOVEMBER

BANG GOES THE NEIGHBOURHOOD

12

In November 1970 a dead whale washed up on a beach in Florence, Oregon. For some obscure reason it fell to the highways department to get rid of it, and George Thornton – who must surely have been a Dad – decided to dynamite it and let scavenging birds do the rest. Against the advice of an explosives expert who happened to be on hand, George used 20 cases of dynamite instead of 20 sticks, and the resulting eruption sent huge chunks of blubber raining down on the large crowd that had gathered to watch, as well as frightening away every scavenging bird for miles around.

HOW MANY?!

13

Lucky old John Hanson of Rayleigh, Essex, today in 1969. Yesterday he had no kids, but today he had five – all girls! His wife Irene had been taking a fertility drug, and it certainly worked as she gave birth to Britain's first surviving set of quins in the 20th century. Little Joanne, Nicola, Julie, Sarah and Jacqueline gave the Hansons an instant basketball team, as well as the prospect of changing over 25,000 nappies in the next two years.

HELLO, AUNTIE

It's often said that the pictures are far better on radio than television, and old-fashioned Dads still like to refer to it as 'the wireless', just to annoy their kids. The British Broadcasting Company went on air today in 1922 from London with Arthur Burrows reading the news, and the following day transmitters in Birmingham and Manchester joined in, informing listeners of developments in that day's general election. 'Auntie' Beeb became a 'Corporation' in December 1926, by which time Lord Reith had begun to insist on radio announcers wearing evening dress when reading the news!

WHAT A ROTTEN BOY

Any Dad who's read the nursery rhyme 'Little Jack Horner' to their kids might want to keep the real story quiet. According to one tradition, Jack (or Thomas) Horner was steward to the Abbot of Glastonbury, Richard Whiting, at the time of Henry VIII. Whiting sent Horner to London to bribe the King with the deeds of 12 manors hidden in a pie. Horner is said to have helped himself to the lucrative manor of Mells – the 'plum'. Horner then sat on a jury that condemned Whiting to death for treason, and the poor cleric was hung, drawn and quartered on Glastonbury Tor today in 1539.

A GRAND DAY OUT

What do education, science and culture have in common? Apart from all making Dads suspicious, they all come under the remit of UNESCO, the preparatory committee of which first met today in 1945. It's the United Nations' body that (among many other things) is in charge of designating World Heritage Sites. There are 24 in the UK, which should be more than enough to fill up a summer holiday, as they range from the Giant's Causeway in Northern Ireland to Stonehenge in England, and from the Pontcysyllte Aqueduct in Wales to St Kilda in Scotland.

CALL THAT A WAR?

Dads love a good war film, but for some reason there's never been a movie made of the Anglo-Swedish War, which broke out today in 1810. That might have something to do with it being the most uneventful war in history: no battles were fought, not even a skirmish, and there were no casualties (if you don't count the poor Swedish farmers killed by their own side when they objected to being conscripted). Sweden, who had previously been allies of the British against France in the Napoleonic Wars, were instructed to declare war by Bonaparte when the little Emperor defeated them – only he never told them they had to do any fighting.

CAN'T YOU COWS JUST TRY AND KEEP IT IN?

18 Kiwi Dads would have felt particularly threatened in 2003 when the New Zealand government, concerned about the greenhouse gas methane, first proposed an 'agricultural emissions research levy' on cattle farmers. Most Antipodeans know how to call a spade a spade, and pretty soon the levy was known as the 'fart tax' and strongly opposed by farmers (and Dads). A 'Fight Against Ridiculous Taxes' movement was formed, and on this day in 2003 they announced the results of their protest poetry competition. In the face of such hardline tactics, it was no surprise when the politicians climbed down.

THERE'S ALWAYS A WORSE DAD THAN YOU

19 In 2002 incompetent Dads all over the world celebrated as Michael Jackson dangled his baby, Prince Michael 'Blanket' Jackson II, from a hotel balcony in Berlin in what the star later admitted was 'a terrible mistake'. Whatever the reason for his bonkers action, from this day on, whenever Mum throws out that old 'You must be the stupidest Dad in the world' line at us, we can point to poor old Jacko: 'OK, I might have left little Jimmy outside the pub, but at least I've never nearly thrown him off a balcony …'

R.I.P.?

What Dad hasn't secretly dreamed of dumping his clothes on a beach, faking his death and shedding his responsibilities? David Nobbs' wonderful creation Reggie Perrin did it in the mid-1970s and, to prove that truth can be stranger than fiction, MP John Stonehouse went first on this day in 1974, leaving a pile of clothes on a Miami beach and departing for a new life in Australia. Apprehended after a few months, Stonehouse was convicted of fraud, theft and forgery and banged up for seven years. Not content with that charge sheet, it was revealed in 2010 that he had been spying for Czech military intelligence!

LET THERE BE LIGHT

US Justice Louis Brandeis said in 1914 that 'sunlight is the best disinfectant' – i.e., people will behave better if they know they can be seen. This theory has been tested to destruction by the UK Parliament, beginning on this day in 1989. When Ian Gow replied to the Queen's Speech he became the first person to make a televised speech in the House of Commons. Those who feared being able to see the behaviour of some MPs would do little for the reputation of Parliament have probably been proved right – but at least our representatives' antics make Dads look more grown-up by comparison.

A LONG WAY DOWN

Plenty of people have parachuted from balloons before now, but when on 14 October 2012 Felix Baumgartner stepped out of his helium-balloon capsule and began to freefall towards the ground there was something different – he was 38km (24 miles) up. On the way down he impressed eight million people watching a live YouTube stream and became the first human to break the sound barrier without being mechanically propelled. Dads suffering from an inferiority complex were probably amused today in 2012 when Felix accepted a BAMBI media award in Germany – and yes, they come in the shape of a cute little fawn. Bless.

PANIC OVER, NOTHING TO SEE

We all scoffed at the preposterous idea that the Large Hadron Collider was going to generate a black hole that would consume the planet, didn't we? And yet it was quite a relief today in 2009 when the first particle collisions took place and we *weren't* all sucked into an enormous void. The particles accelerate around a tunnel 27km (17 miles) in circumference that crosses the Franco-Swiss border four times, but they never have to show their passports. And which sailor works at the LHC, Dad? Bosun Higgs!

CRISIS? WHAT CRISIS?

OK, the Suez Crisis was a bit of a flap and it did bring down Prime Minister Anthony Eden, but look on the bright side. If you were a Dad struggling to pass your driving test in 1956, from today you could tootle around on your own, as tests were suspended and would remain so until April 1957. The downside was that you probably hadn't got any petrol to drive anywhere, as all the Ministry of Transport driving examiners were taken off tests to administer petrol rationing. You can't win.

WISE WORDS

Albert Einstein knew a bit about relativity and gravity, and he presented his theories – what are now known as the Einstein Field Equations – to the Prussian Academy of Sciences today in 1915.

He also knew a bit about Dads, if one quote attributed to him is anything to go by. 'Two things are infinite,' he said, 'the universe and human stupidity ... and I'm not sure about the universe.'

KEEP A STIFF UPPER LIP

Dads are renowned for burying their feelings so deep you couldn't find them with a fleet of JCBs. And who and what epitomises that more than Trevor Howard in *Brief Encounter* (released today in 1945)? When he fell in love with a married woman, did he make a big song and dance about it? When he realised it was doomed, did he confess all on Mumsnet? When he was robbed of the chance for even a farewell kiss, did he stamp his feet? No, he damn well didn't. He got on the train meekly, and, if he was your typical Dad, had probably forgotten all about it by the time he got home.

HOOK, LINE AND SINKER

We've already seen how Dads like a practical joke (see 2 February). Theodore Hook was keen on them too, and his most famous took place today in 1810, when he arranged for dozens and dozens of tradesmen, merchants, doctors, lawyers, priests and, finally, distinguished dignitaries such as the Lord Mayor of London and the Archbishop of Canterbury to call on a Mrs Tottenham of Berners Street. It was all to win a bet that he could make any house in London the most talked-about address in town within a week. And it worked – mayhem ensued and the street was at a standstill for the whole day.

FREEDOM OF THE PRESS

Even though many newspapers are now free online, the actual physical version remains indispensable to Dads, a thin but impermeable barrier he can erect over the cornflakes to avoid the battles of breakfast. And this essential aid became available to the masses from today in 1814 when the first copies of *The Times* to be printed on Friedrich Koenig's new steam-powered press were sold. The printing press had been around since 1439, but it was when it was harnessed to the all-powerful steam that its potential really took off.

27 YEARS IN THE TUB

It's holiday time in Liberia today, as the West African country celebrates William Tubman's Birthday. Tubman, born this day in 1895, is known as the 'father of modern Liberia'. He was the longest-serving president of this unusual country, 'back-colonised' in the 1820s by freed African-American slaves. And now you know who he is, I can tell you this joke. Tubman: 'Why do you keep bringing me all these books?' 'I'm sorry, I thought you said you were a librarian.'

GENUINE HENS' TEETH FOR SALE

Today in 1968 the Trades' Descriptions Act came into force and shoppers could do something if they thought they were being taken for a ride. Early complaints included an 'undetectable' toupee that wasn't, some 'washable' trousers that weren't, and a 'ninepence cup of coffee' that somehow cost one and threepence (that's 6½p – what a ripoff!). Dads are always trying to convince their kids of stuff, like the word 'gullible' being taken out of the dictionary. Maybe there should be a Dads' Descriptions Act …

DECEMBER

DIVINE WIND?

 Which is what some Dads think karaoke means in Japanese, or at least you'd think that to hear them perform. Of course, divine wind is *kamikaze*, and *karaoke* is 'empty orchestra', often leading to an 'empty room'. Hugely popular in Japan and the rest of the Far East, you will be unsurprised to learn that there are karaoke world championships. The 2012 male and female champions, Luis Boutin and Raquel Pando, were crowned in Lappeeranta, Finland, on this day. Perhaps they should have been accompanied by the Air Guitar World Champion (see 30 August) – the Lapps obviously have a thing for strange musical contests.

BARINGS GO BUST

Dads are traditionally suspicious of banks and bankers, so might have had a wry smile when 'rogue trader' Nick Leeson bankrupted Barings, Britain's oldest merchant bank, and was then sent to prison for fraud today in 1995. Leeson had been Barings' chief futures trader in Singapore, and at first made good profits. But when he had a bad run he hid the losses and threw good money after bad in a desperate attempt to cover his tracks; by the time he realised the game was up and left a pathetic 'I'm sorry' note on his desk, he'd cost the bank £860m.

IT'S NEVER TOO LATE (2)

If cricketing Dads under 50 can still nurture hopes of an international call-up (see 3 June), those with a penchant for crooning have got another decade before they give up on making the hit parade. Today in 1963 the great Louis Armstrong recorded 'Hello Dolly!' prior to the musical of the same name opening the following month. He was 62, and nearer 63 when the record hit the top spot on the *Billboard* charts in May 1964, making him the oldest artist ever to have a number one. Well done, Satchmo!

DECEMBER

COW PIES ALL ROUND

Dads are always sneaking a peek at their kids' comics, and the Daddy of all British comics was surely the *Dandy*, which was first published today in 1937. It stood out in its early days for being one of the few comics to use speech balloons in the pictures rather than captions below them. The *Dandy* ran in print until this day in 2012, when it bowed to the inevitable decline in sales and went to online editions. At its peak in the 1950s it was selling two million copies a week, with favourite characters Korky the Cat and Desperate Dan keeping nippers entertained.

CHEERS!

A great day for American Dads as the 21st Amendment to the US Constitution was ratified in 1933, repealing the 18th Amendment of 1920 that banned alcohol. The 13 intervening years had seen drinking and crime rise and respect for the law fall. None of the benefits promised by the temperance movement materialised, and the government found itself spending a lot of money trying to enforce a law that hardly anybody obeyed, all without the benefit of alcohol taxes. It was inevitable that Prohibition would end, although some states chose to remain officially dry – Mississippi did so until the 1960s!

A SMELLIE LEGACY

Today in 1768 the very first edition of *Encyclopedia Britannica* was published in Edinburgh under the editorship of William Smellie. It grew into the most renowned general reference source in the world, and by the time of its final print edition in 2012 it stretched to 32 volumes and 40 million words. Its operators have now acknowledged the impossible task of keeping a large-volume printwork up to date in the 21st century, and future editions will be online only. Dads, of course, have no need of encyclopedias – their kids know everything already!

GEORGE HOLDS UP FRED

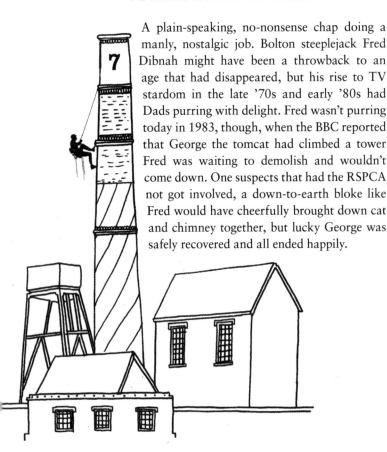

A plain-speaking, no-nonsense chap doing a manly, nostalgic job. Bolton steeplejack Fred Dibnah might have been a throwback to an age that had disappeared, but his rise to TV stardom in the late '70s and early '80s had Dads purring with delight. Fred wasn't purring today in 1983, though, when the BBC reported that George the tomcat had climbed a tower Fred was waiting to demolish and wouldn't come down. One suspects that had the RSPCA not got involved, a down-to-earth bloke like Fred would have cheerfully brought down cat and chimney together, but lucky George was safely recovered and all ended happily.

IT COULD HAPPEN TO ANYONE

Dads know how easy it is to get things the wrong way round, so would have been delighted to have proof of this today in 2005. A trainee trader at Mizuho Bank in Tokyo had a deceptively simple task – sell one share in J-com, a company that was new to the market, at 610,000 yen. Instead he attempted to sell 610,000 shares at one yen each; if the trade could have been fulfilled it would have lost Mizuho $3bn. Luckily, J-com only had 15,000 shares, so losses were limited to a measly $223m. Phew!

THE UMPIRE IS ALWAYS RIGHT ...

... even when he's wrong. Dads have instilled this into their offspring down the ages, and without this principle sport would collapse into anarchy. But it was stretched to breaking point today in 1987 as England's cricket tour to Pakistan threatened to collapse. England captain Mike Gatting had lost his temper as yet another decision went against his team, muttering that it was 'one rule for one, one for another', and he and Pakistan umpire Shakoor Rana ended up wagging fingers at one another – it doesn't get much stronger than that in cricket! Gatting backed down to save the tour, but the damage to cricket's reputation was done.

THAT'S AN OLD ONE

In the 1940s scientist Willard Libby was part of the team working on the development of the US atomic bomb. In 1945 he moved to the University of Chicago and developed the theories around the use of carbon-14 (radiocarbon) to accurately date organic matter. This was a great boon for the field of archaeology and on this day in 1960 Libby received the Nobel Prize for Chemistry for his work. In 2012 some flutes made of bone and ivory were carbon-dated to between 42,000 and 43,000 years old – that's almost as old as Dads' jokes!

WE LOVE ERNIE (2)

What a great year for pop-pickers 1971 was. Artists to hit number one in the UK included George Harrison, T. Rex (twice), Diana Ross and Rod Stewart. Strangely though, the year was topped and tailed by a couple of novelty records, opening with Clive Dunn's 'Granddad' and closing with Dads' favourite 'Ernie' by Benny Hill, which knocked Slade off the top spot on this day. The tragic tale of the fastest milkman in the west, his horse Trigger and his nemesis Two Ton Ted the baker, was Christmas number one and has been a favourite ever since. According to Wikipedia the song was 'innuendo-laden', but I think that's just their dirty minds.

HE AIN'T HEAVY

Today in 1917 Father Edward J. Flanagan opened the first Boys' Town orphanage in the city of Omaha, Nebraska. He wanted to run a new type of home for boys without Dads of their own, to give them responsibility and prepare them to become good citizens. His work inspired the 1938 Spencer Tracy film *Boys' Town*. In 1943 Boys' Town adopted as a logo a picture of an older boy carrying a younger boy on his back, captioned, 'He ain't heavy, mister, he's my brother', which inspired the Hollies hit written by Bobby Scott and Bob Russell.

THE TIMESAVER

To hear the ladies going on, you'd think they were the only ones who had decisions to make when getting dressed. But it's harder for formally dressed Dads. First we have to decide which cartoon tie to wear today: Mickey, Homer, Roadrunner ... the choice is endless. Then we have to think about the knot: do we go for the full Windsor or the half-Windsor? Or perhaps the four-in-hand? It doesn't help having Mum in the background suggesting the Pratt. So if you're running late, say a quick thank-you to whoever invented the clip-on tie today in 1928, and bung one of them on.

DECEMBER

UP, UP AND AWAY

1970s Dads had a bit of a thing for the Nimble bread girl in the TV adverts – that combination of a pretty, wholesome young woman in a balloon, flying over beautiful British countryside, and all with the prospect of a bacon butty at the end of it. The very first test flight of a hot-air balloon took place today in 1782. Fortunately it was unmanned, as after floating for 2km (1¼ miles), it was destroyed on landing. By the following year inventors the Montgolfier brothers had refined their design and the first manned flight took place.

THE HEIDI GAME

American Dads would have been on the edge of their seats today in 1968. The New York Jets were leading the Oakland Raiders in a thrilling football game that was lasting longer than expected. Still, there were just a few minutes to go … when at 7pm, promptly, TV cut away from the game to show the big film, *Heidi*. Sports fans missed the two late scores that turned the game in Oakland's favour, and went ballistic. In fairness, network executives had tried to phone the station to tell them to stay with the game, but the switchboard was jammed with viewers ringing up to ask if they were going to stay with the game!

THE KING NEEDS BURPING

When Henry VI's Dad (Henry V) died in 1422 Henry became England's youngest ever king – he was nine months old. And when his Granddad (Charles VI) died two months later, the tiny tot became King of France as well. He had to grow up quickly, and when a rival to the French throne crowned himself Charles VII in July 1429, on 16 December that year eight-year-old Henry had *his* official coronation in Paris. In 1453 the English were driven out of most of France for good, although they held Calais for another century.

WHAT A CARRY ON

Released today in 1964 with a tagline of 'The funniest film since 54 BC', *Carry On Cleo* had a lot to live up to. Fortunately this classic instalment of probably the most successful comedy series in British film history did just that. With characters like Senna Pod, Sosages and the entrepreneurs Marcus and Spencius, it was a typical *Carry On* combination of slapstick and innuendo that Dads can't resist, but with an additional dash of wit that placed it ahead of all its fellows, with the possible exception of the brilliant *Carry On Up The Khyber.*

'DID WE WIN?'

Dads are always being accused of being behind the times, but by 1974 most of them had realised that World War Two was over. Not so Teruo Nakamura, who on this day became the last of the Japanese 'holdouts' to be discovered when he was arrested by Indonesian soldiers on Morotai island. He had been declared dead in March 1945 and then teamed up with other stragglers for a few years before striking out on his own. On learning that *Desert Island Discs* was still going strong (see 11 May), he asked to be sent back to his home-made hut.

HIS FACE LOOKS FAMILIAR

On 5 December 2013 Nelson Mandela died; the world grieved, and India announced five days of national mourning. A clothmaker from Chennai had a huge billboard erected, declaring: 'We should be proud we were part of an era when they lived,' with images of Gandhi, Mother Teresa and Martin Luther King, and a large picture of ... Morgan Freeman, who played Mandela in *Invictus* in 2009. Today in 2013 the Twittersphere was filled with snaps of the embarrassing billboard. Dads who have bluffed their way through parents' evenings without having a clue which teacher is which would have sympathised.

IT'S A WONDERFUL LIFE

This heart-warming film that has become a staple of the Christmas season was released today in 1946. Directed by Frank Capra and starring James Stewart, it tells the story of George Bailey, a Dad of four who is on the verge of suicide. Guardian angel Clarence Odbody (still an apprentice angel after 200 years!) appears to talk him out of it by showing him the bad things that would have happened had he never been born. George sees that his life hasn't been wasted, Clarence wins his wings, and everybody goes 'Aaaahh'.

ARMAGEDDON OUT OF HERE

Good news for Dads today in 2012 when the world didn't end. Cynics among you will point out that it didn't end on every other day too, but that's just splitting hairs. The Mayan calendar said it would end today and it didn't. It turned out in May 2012 that archaeologists had found a missing piece of the Mayan calendar – in the same way Dads find the last jigsaw pieces down the back of the sofa – that showed it going on and on forever, but it was still a relief when 22 December arrived and we were still here.

AS FAST AS YOU LIKE

When I was a boy my Dad used to tell me that the 'unrestricted' speed signs of a black diagonal on a white circle meant you could go 'as fast as you like'. I only found out later that it actually meant the 'national speed limit' of 70mph (112kph).

Mind you, in the cars Dad had at the time, he was probably right – we could go as fast we liked and would never reach 70. But before today in 1965, when the 70mph limit was introduced, you *could* go at any speed on unrestricted roads – it's been 60mph (96kph) for single-carriageway roads since 1977.

BEECHING IS CUT

We've already seen in several entries that Dads have a soft spot for railways, so they would have been cheering today in 1964 when it was announced that Dr Richard Beeching was leaving British Rail – sacked or resigned it was never quite clear. By then, though, the damage had been done – Beeching had recommended and overseen the closure of almost 13,000km (8,000 miles) of track and 2,000 stations. Maybe it was necessary surgery by the doctor – though many railwaymen will never be convinced – but it was certainly good news in the future for cyclists and walkers, as many disused railways became tranquil paths.

WHERE'S SANTA?

A Dad's most important job on Christmas Eve is to be able to tell his kids where in the world Father Christmas is at any given time – it's vital for getting the little beggars into bed early. And he's had help since Christmas Eve 1955, when a newspaper ad telling kids to ring Santa printed the wrong number. As a result, children got through to the Continental Aerospace Command Center (CONAD, later NORAD) hotline. Colonel Harry Shoup inspiringly appointed himself Head Elf and told staff to give callers the current location for Santa, a tradition that has continued to this day; now we can all track Santa online thanks to NORAD.

A GOODIE OR A BADDIE?

Today in 1076 Boleslaw II was crowned King of Poland. Dads will love the fact that he's the only king that rhymes with coleslaw (don't bother telling him it's probably pronounced *Boll-esh-lav*, he won't be interested) and that he had three nicknames (see 7 September): the Generous, the Bold and the Cruel. He produced his own coinage (generous) and murdered a bishop (cruel), but if he'd been cautious instead of bold he might have lived longer – he was apparently poisoned in around 1082.

I HAVE A SONG TO SING-O!

There's a certain type of Dad that baffles his kids by wandering around the house singing about having 'a little list' or being 'a Pirate King' or 'the very model of a modern major-general'. He's a fan of Gilbert and Sullivan, the Rice and Lloyd-Webber of their day, whose 14 comic operas are still performed with more enthusiasm than skill to this day. The combination of Gilbert's witty words and Sullivan's catchy music made them both a fortune, and today in 1871 their first collaboration, *Thespis*, opened at the Gaiety Theatre.

'I AM YOUR FATHER'

Most kids come to realise pretty quickly that Dad is their arch-enemy, but what a shock to discover that your arch-enemy is really your Dad! That's what happens to Luke Skywalker in the *Star Wars* trilogy, the first episode of which was released in the UK today in 1977. It had been out since May in the US, so anticipation was high after seven months of hype and publicity. Thousands braved the cold weather to queue outside cinemas – and the BBC even reported ticket touts cashing in, with advance £2.20 tickets going for £30. Dad joke: What did Obi-Wan say when he saw Luke eating pie with a spoon? Use the fork, Luke!

PATHETIC POET

Today in 1879 the Tay Bridge in Scotland collapsed and a train plunged into the river, killing all 75 on board. It was commemorated in a poem written by William Topaz McGonagall, now celebrated as probably the worst poet in the history of English literature (there's a target for ditty-coining Dads). The 'orrible ode contained lines like: 'So the train mov'd slowly along the Bridge of Tay/ Until it was about midway/ Then the central girders with a crash gave way/ And down went the train and passengers into the Tay!' They don't write 'em like that any more.

NATIONAL TREASURE

Bernard Cribbins' career is a cascade of programmes and films Dads love to watch with their kids: *The Railway Children*, *The Wombles*, *Jackanory*, *Doctor Who* … he was the guest storyteller on *Jackanory* on more occasions than anyone else, with 114 appearances. He's also appeared in *Carry On* films, *Fawlty Towers*, had comedy-song hits with 'Hole in the Ground' and 'Right Said Fred', and even voiced Tufty the Squirrel in the road-safety campaigns of the 1960s and '70s. He received a long-overdue OBE in 2011. And today's his birthday (born 1928). Many happy returns, Bernard.

DECEMBER

NO MISTAKE WITH MICHAEL

We all make mistakes, especially Dads, so what a boon it was when correction fluid was invented. We might know it best as Tippex, but its creator Bette Nesmith Graham called it 'Mistake Out' when she began to market it after using it herself for five years working as a secretary. It was rebranded Liquid Paper and she sold the business in 1979 for $47.5m. But correction fluid wasn't Bette's only significant production. On this day in 1942 she gave birth to a son, Michael Nesmith, who found fame with the Monkees.

IT'S A BIT DARK IN HERE

Dads don't like paying bills of any kind, and one of their least favourite is the tax bill. So it's a good job we haven't still got the Window Tax, which was introduced today in 1695. Seen as a tax on light and air and hugely unpopular (not least with glaziers), it led to changes in building design to reduce the number of windows, and many large houses with lots of windows had some bricked up, waiting for the day the tax was repealed (they had a long wait – until 1851). Some believe this tax was the origin of the phrase 'daylight robbery'.